Pay-Off Pitch

The Chip Hilton Sports Series

For more information on
Chip Hilton-related activities and to correspond
with other Chip Hilton fans, check the website at
www.chiphilton.com

Chip Hilton Sports Series
#16

Pay-Off Pitch

Coach Clair Bee

Updated by Randall and Cynthia Bee Farley

Foreword by Jack McCallum

BROADMAN
& HOLMAN
PUBLISHERS

Nashville, Tennessee

© 2000 by Randall K. and Cynthia Bee Farley
All rights reserved
Printed in the United States of America

0-8054-2095-9

Published by Broadman & Holman Publishers,
Nashville, Tennessee

Subject Heading: BASEBALL—FICTION / YOUTH
Library of Congress Card Catalog Number: 00-023654

Library of Congress Cataloging-in-Publication Data
Bee, Clair.
    Pay-off pitch / written by Clair Bee ; updated by Cynthia Bee
Farley & Randall Farley.
        p. cm. — (Chip Hilton sports series; #16)
    Summary: As a member of the college baseball team at
State University, Chip Hilton finds his sense of sportsmanship
challenged when he is wrongfully suspected of playing for a
professional team.
    ISBN 0-8054-2095-9 (tp)
    [1. Baseball—Fiction. 2. Sportsmanship—Fiction. 3. Colleges
and universities—Fiction.] I. Farley, Cynthia Bee, 1952– .
II. Farley, Randall K., 1952– . III. Title.

PZ7.B38196Pay   2000
[Fic]—dc21
                                      00-023654
                                          CIP

1 2 3 4 5 04 03 02 01 00

"The rigid volunteer rules
of right and wrong in sports
are second only to religious faith in moral training . . .
and baseball is the greatest of American sports."
—HERBERT HOOVER

CLAIR BEE, 1957

TO

CHICK SCIPLE AND DR. PAULA CONNOLLY
With gratitude for your inspiration.

RANDY AND CINDY
2000

Contents

CONTENTS

Foreword

IT'S SOMETIMES difficult to figure out why we became who we became. Was it an influential teacher who steered you toward biology? A beloved grandparent who turned you into a machinist? A motorcycle accident that forced you into accounting?

All I know is that in my case the Chip Hilton books had something—no, a lot—to do with my becoming a sports journalist. At the very least, the books got me to sit down and read when others of my generation were watching television or otherwise goofing off; at most, they taught me many of life's lessons, about sports and sportsmanship, about coaches and coaching, about winning and losing.

Also, the books helped me, quite literally, get the job I have now. Over two decades ago, when I was a sportswriter at a small newspaper in Pennsylvania, I interviewed Clair Bee and wrote a piece about him and the Hilton books. For some strange reason, even before I met

FOREWORD

Clair, I knew I could make the story memorable, knew that meeting a legend like Clair and plumbing his mind for memories were going to be magic. They were. I sold the story to *Sports Illustrated,* and, partly because of it, I was later hired there full time.

To my surprise, and especially to the surprise of the editors at *SI,* the story produced a torrent of letters, hundreds of them, all written by closet Clair and Chip fans who, like me, had grown up on the books and never been able to forget them. Since the piece about Clair appeared in 1979, I've written hundreds of other articles, many of them cover stories about famous athletes like Michael Jordan, Magic Johnson, and Larry Bird; yet I'm still known, by and large, as the "guy who wrote the Chip Hilton story." I would safely say that still, two decades later, six months do not go by that I don't receive some kind of question about Clair and Chip.

One of the many fortunate things that happened to me as a result of that story was meeting Clair's daughter, Cindy Farley, and her husband, Randy, as well as others who could recite the starting lineups of Coach Rockwell's Valley Falls teams.

I am proud to have played a small part in the revival of Chip and the restoration of interest in Clair (not that real basketball people ever forget him). It's hard to put a finger on what exactly endures from the books, but it occurs to me that what Clair succeeded in doing was to create a universe of which we would all like to be a part.

As I leafed through one of the books recently, a memory came back to me from my days as a twelve-year-old Pop Warner football player in Mays Landing, New Jersey. A friend who shared my interest in the books had just thrown an opposing quarterback for a loss in a key

FOREWORD

game. As we walked back to the huddle, he put his arm on my shoulder pads and, conjuring up a Hilton gang character, whispered, "Another jarring tackle by Biggie Cohen." No matter how old you get, you never forget something like that. Thank you, Clair Bee.

JACK McCALLUM
Senior Writer, *Sports Illustrated*

CHAPTER 1

Blue Caps and Socks

CHIP HILTON folded the long fingers of his right hand into a fist and thumped it into the pocket of his glove. "Look at that," he breathed, nudging the freckled-faced guy with red hair who stood beside him.

"I'm lookin'," Soapy Smith replied in a weak voice. "What is this, a big-league training camp?"

State's big field house was as full of action as Washington, D.C.'s, Union Station at lunchtime! At the far end of the giant structure, State's varsity baseball candidates were loosening up, playing catch and pepper ball. The lettermen were dressed in gray uniforms with blue socks and caps. The rest of the hopefuls, sophomores for the most part, wore gray uniforms with red socks and caps.

The track team was practicing in the opposite end of the big indoor arena, while candidates for the tennis team were receiving instructions on a special court along the right side of the building.

PAY-OFF PITCH

"A lot of blue caps out there," Soapy whispered, glancing up at his tall, serious-faced friend. He waited for Chip's reaction and then continued anxiously. "There must be at least thirty."

"There's lots of red ones too."

"We can handle the red ones," Soapy said significantly, fingering the red cap he held in his right hand.

Soapy had something there. He and Chip knew all about the players in the red caps; they had played with them on State's freshman team the previous year when State University had begun its NCAA pilot program. The two lifelong friends had made a formidable battery for the "Fence Busters," last year's freshman team. The team had caught everyone by surprise, and these players "knew the score" when it came to the sophomore competition. But beating out a letterman for a regular job on the varsity . . . Well, that was something else altogether.

The two stood quietly, side by side, each busy with his own thoughts. Chip gently rubbed his right elbow with his gloved hand and looked for the rest of his hometown friends, Biggie Cohen, Red Schwartz, and Speed Morris. There they were—three red caps among a sea of red in the corner. Biggie Cohen towered above everyone in sight. The big first baseman was playing catch with Fireball Finley, one of Chip's and Soapy's friends and a coworker at Grayson's, a popular gathering place for the college crowd.

Three men, also wearing baseball uniforms, leaned against a batting cage and watched the proceedings. The tallest of the three was State's head baseball coach, Del Bennett. The head coach was a former major-league player, and his renown as a college mentor was known throughout the country.

"We've been waiting a long time for this," Chip murmured. "Imagine! A big-league star for a coach."

BLUE CAPS AND SOCKS

Soapy followed the direction of Chip's glance and nodded in agreement. "Remember when we first saw him? The time we visited campus, and he showed you how to pitch?"

"I'll never forget it," Chip said simply.

There was a short silence while the two boys continued to survey the busy scene. Chip didn't let on to Soapy, but he was worried about his knee. A strained ligament had handicapped him all through basketball season. He was wondering now whether it would be the same thing all over again! His knee was still tight, and he didn't have his usual speed, but the pain was gone. "Well, I'll soon find out," he muttered.

"What did you say, Chip?"

"Nothing, Soapy," Chip shook his head and grinned. "I was just thinking out loud."

Chip shifted his glance to the shorter, stockier man in the group and a brief, warm smile played across the young player's lips. Henry Rockwell was Del Bennett's first assistant, but he meant a lot more than that to Chip and the rest of the guys. Rockwell had coached them during their high school days and had retired from Valley Falls High School the same year Chip, Soapy, Biggie, Red, and Speed graduated. And like Chip and the rest of the Valley Falls crew, this was Rock's second year at State.

"Well," Chip said briskly, glancing at Soapy's red cap, "I guess we'd better get going. We've got to convince Coach Bennett that we need some new equipment."

"New equipment? What kind of equipment?"

"Oh, blue caps and socks—stuff like that!"

A broad smile broke across Soapy's face, and his eyes brightened. "Yes!" he agreed enthusiastically. "That's right! Blue's our favorite color."

PAY-OFF PITCH

Coach Bennett's shrill whistle interrupted them just then. Chip and Soapy followed the other candidates to the small bleacher section behind the batting cage. The tall coach waited until the players were seated and then stepped out in front of the squad. "I imagine most of you know that I'm Del Bennett," he said, smiling, "and that the gentleman on my right is Henry Rockwell, my associate."

"Assistant," Rockwell said, smiling that crooked smile of his that always made Chip feel everything was right with the world.

Del Bennett nodded and hooked a thumb toward the man on his left. "And this is Jim Corrigan, our freshman coach. He'll be with us until the freshmen report. The three of us are supposed to teach you enough baseball to win one or two games."

"Better not *lose* more than two," one of the blue caps whispered.

Bennett smiled briefly and continued. "This could be our big year. Our year to win the conference, maybe the NCAA championship. We have a lot of lettermen back and a lot of fine players up from last year's freshman team. We could go a long way—maybe all the way."

"Lot of players is right," Chip mused to himself as he studied the candidates. His mind was working with great speed. Hector "Hex" Rickard was *his* big rival. Hex had experience and was a good prospect for major league baseball, and he was a strong leader. The tall senior was surrounded by a group of veterans. Rod "Diz" Dean and Terrell "Flash" Sparks had pitched freshman ball with Chip the year before. Chip knew their potential. They were sitting with the sophomore group.

Edwin "Doogie" Dugan was an unknown entity. But Wilder, State's regular catcher, and Al Engle, who had made up a junior college battery with Dugan the previous year, seemed to think the little pitcher had a lot on the ball. Wilder, Engle, Dugan, and several varsity veterans were sitting together in the top row of bleachers. *Three groups,* Chip thought to himself. *That could mean trouble.*

Chip thought about Soapy, and he glanced at Mitch "Widow" Wilder. The veteran catcher was sure of the call as the regular receiver. Soapy was good, but he didn't have Wilder's experience. Chip shifted his attention to Al Engle. The junior college graduate had all the attributes of a good catcher too.

"Time will tell," Chip mused.

Coach Bennett looked out the window at the steady sheet of rain coming down. He shook his head "We've got just three weeks to get ready for our first game. And a word of advice about your chief asset—a good arm.

"Ballplayers aren't born with glass arms. They usually acquire them by showing off or by throwing too hard. Too soon. These damp, rainy days are bad for arms. So take care of your arms by warming up thoroughly every day.

"All right, let's have some calisthenics. Fall in! Three lines, arm's length apart."

Chip lined up between Soapy and Biggie, with Speed and Red and Fireball in the same line. Coach Bennett led the drill, starting with an arm exercise and counting the rhythm aloud.

"One-two-three-four! One-two-three-four and halt!" It was a tough coordination drill, and Chip gave it all he had, thinking that Del Bennett had to be in great shape to set such a pace. The coach was breathing evenly when he stopped.

"All right," Bennett said, "now let's have a few deep knee bends." He paused until he located Chip. "You'd better skip this one, Hilton. On the count of four, every-body. Ready—"

Chip pretended not to notice the curious glances directed his way and instead gave the knee-bending a try. The result was a clumsy effort, but it enabled him to hide his flushed face. The next drill was a set of ten fast push-ups; these were easy. He had no more difficulty with the exercises and was still going strong when Bennett ended with twenty fast trunk bends.

"All right," Bennett called. "Not bad for a start! Now, let's have a little pepper ball and throwing to loosen up our arms."

While the candidates worked out, the three coaches stood in front of the bleachers and quietly watched the players' efforts. To the casual eye, the three men were taking it easy, but that was far from true. They were appraising each player, discussing his background, experience, and potential value to the team.

"Those two kids who just completed junior college are supposed to be pretty good," Bennett commented.

"You mean Dugan and Engle?"

Bennett nodded. "Engle looks like a pretty good catching prospect, but Dugan seems a little small for a pitcher."

"He is a little small," Rockwell acknowledged, "but you never can tell. By the way, we've got plenty of strength behind the plate. Maybe too much."

"You can never have too many receivers, Rock. Especially if they can hit. I was watching Rickard. He looks good. He's the only *real* pitcher back from last year. He and Hilton will have to carry the pitching load, unless those other two kids you had on the freshman team last year can help."

"Dean and Sparks?"

"That's right." Bennett hesitated. "But what about Hilton? Is that knee trouble he ran into in basketball going to slow him up?"

Rockwell's reply was a long time coming. His sharp, black eyes were focused on the tall, blond athlete toeing the practice rubber and firing the ball at his redheaded buddy. Rockwell turned back to the head coach, his thin lips breaking into a crooked smile. "He might be a little slow on the base paths, Del, but that's all."

"And his arm?"

Rockwell nodded toward Chip. "Take a look," he said softly.

Bennett watched the smooth, effortless sweep of Chip's long arm. "I see what you mean," he said, grinning in approval.

Chip's arm had been in top shape the very first day of practice. With Soapy's big glove providing the target, Chip and the redhead had been playing catch for three weeks. If Coach Bennett called for squad work, Chip felt ready and strong enough to pitch a full game.

After practice, Chip and Soapy walked across the campus and down Main Street until they reached Grayson's. On the way, they talked baseball. Chip, Soapy, and Fireball had all worked for Mr. Grayson in his store since the year before. Their interest in the game carried beyond the diamond; they talked baseball while working late nights and in their dorm rooms at Jefferson Hall before they fell asleep. Jeff Hall was home to the Valley Falls crew and a number of other sophomore friends, and there were always people to talk baseball with.

Friday morning, exactly one week after the first baseball workout, Soapy lifted his head for a quick look out the window and then leaped from his bed.

"Sunshine!" he yelped delightedly. "Excellent! Now we can play a little baseball!"

That afternoon the very air seemed to be charged with the players' enthusiasm. Coach Bennett and Henry Rockwell liked what they saw and went right to work. First, everyone loosened up with calisthenics. Next, everyone practiced base-running, and then it was time for the sliding pit. Chip got into line in front of the sliding pit too. But when his turn came, Coach Bennett stopped him. "No you don't, Hilton. Drop out."

Al Engle and Doogie Dugan were in line behind Chip and took advantage of the opportunity to take a shot at Hilton. "Lots of delicate little flowers bloom in the spring, Doogie," Engle muttered softly, nudging his pal, Widow Wilder.

"Shhh," Wilder hissed. "That's the basketball star, Chip Hilton."

Chip darted a glance at them and started to speak. But he was too late. Engle took off at full speed and threw himself into a reckless hook slide.

"Nice going!" Bennett called enthusiastically. "That's the way to come into the bag. Tear it off the peg. All right! Come on, Dugan."

The little pitcher sped toward the pit and came into the bag with a beautiful fall-away slide. Widow Wilder followed with the same wild abandon, and then the three friends walked slowly back toward the end of the line, passing Chip on the way.

Chip eyed the three quizzically. Just as they passed, Dugan taunted him again. "Coach saving you for the May Day dance, Hilton?"

Before Chip could answer, Wilder good-naturedly elbowed the pint-sized pitcher and winked at Chip.

BLUE CAPS AND SOCKS

"Don't mind Doogie," he said, grinning. "He's practicing up on his bench-jockeying."

Following sliding and the usual group work, Bennett electrified every player on the field when he bellowed a final command. "On the double now! Red caps, take the field! Send Hilton and Smith out here, Rock. Cohen, you take first base; Gillen, second; Durley, third; Morris, shortstop; Finley, Burke, and Schwartz in the outfield. Blue caps, hit in this order: Ryder, Crowell, Harris, Wilder, Bentley, Carter, Reed, Merton, and Rickard. Let's go!"

While Soapy was strapping on his shin guards and chest protector, Chip walked slowly out to the mound, deep in thought. *This is it! This is your first real test as a college pitcher. Now you'll find out for sure how good you are.*

Soapy had approached unheard. "All right, Chipper?" he asked nervously. "Are you all right?"

Chip nodded. "Sure, Soapy. Right as I'll ever be."

"Same old signs?"

Chip nodded once more. "Same old signs, Soapy."

Soapy thumped a fist into his big glove and nodded aggressively. "We'll kill 'em!" he said belligerently, turning back to the plate.

Ted "Tubby" Ryder, the first hitter for the blue caps, was short and stocky, batted righty, and crowded the plate. Soapy called for a fastball, low and inside, and Chip's pitch smacked into the redhead's big glove for a called strike. Chip breathed a sigh of relief. Now he was ahead of the hitter. He kept ahead and struck Ryder out on a curveball and then another fastball.

Ozzie "The Whiz" Crowell took a look at the first pitch, a ball, and topped the second pitch straight back to the mound. Chip took it on the first hop and fired the ball to Biggie for an easy out. Two away! That brought up Reggie Harris, Biggie Cohen's first-base rival, and Chip set him down swinging on three fast ones, all around the wrists.

Biggie, Speed, Soapy, and the rest of the red caps came running off the field to surround Chip before he reached the dugout. "Nothing to it!" Soapy chortled.

Soapy was right. Chip pitched for three innings, setting the blue caps down without a hit and striking out five hitters. Not a batter reached first base. It was clear that he was far and away ahead of the blue-cap hitters. Hex Rickard was almost as good, pitching for another three, although Biggie bounced one of the lefty's fast ones off the right-field fence for a three-bagger. Neither team scored during the six innings, and Coach Bennett sent both Chip and Rickard to the showers.

Engle and Dugan replaced Rickard and Wilder with the blue caps, and Darrin Nickels and Diz Dean took over for the red caps. Soapy and Widow Wilder were assigned to coaching-box duties.

While the new pitchers were warming up, Bennett joined Rockwell and Corrigan beside the batting cage. There was a pleased gleam in his eyes as he watched Chip and Rickard walk through the gate beside the grandstand. "What a pair," he said.

"Not bad for college," Corrigan agreed.

"Not bad!" Rockwell echoed. "You can say that again."

"I may be wrong," Bennett said significantly, "but right now I think those are two of the best college pitchers I ever saw." He slapped Rockwell on the back. "We've got the best one-two pitching punch in the conference, Hank."

But when the head coach called off practice an hour later and joined Rockwell and Corrigan in the coaches' locker room, the excitement had disappeared. Bennett slumped down on a bench, rubbing his head with his hands.

"Well, what do you think?" Corrigan asked.

"I don't know," Bennett replied slowly. "Stacks up as the best squad we've had here in years."

"But—" Rockwell prompted.

"But," Bennett said worriedly, "a lot of fine teams have been ruined by cliques."

CHAPTER 2

A Ballplayer's Player

MITCH "WIDOW" WILDER was keenly enjoying razzing his two friends. "What kind of a ball were you seeing out there this afternoon, Doogie?" he asked Dugan.

"What kind do you think?" Dugan retorted quickly. "A round ball."

"I thought it was a soccer ball," Wilder said innocently.

"Coach said not to use anything but straight stuff, Widow," Engle remonstrated.

Wilder grunted. "That's all Hilton used."

"So what?" Dugan shrugged.

"Well, I didn't see anyone getting a piece of it," Wilder retorted.

Dugan grinned. "That includes you, man," he said. "I noticed he had you fanning the breeze."

"You're right, he did," the big catcher said quietly. "And that's why I'm out to cultivate Hilton's friendship."

"Friendship?" Dugan repeated incredulously. "Why would you want him for a friend?"

"I've got a good reason."

"What kind of a reason?" Dugan persisted.

"One of the best. Money! Hilton's going to make me some money."

"I don't get it," Engle said.

Wilder grinned snidely. "No? Well, this is in confidence. Just between us three. OK?"

"Sure. Go ahead," Engle said. "You know where we stand."

"Right," Dugan echoed. "Go ahead."

"OK. You guys think I know my baseball?"

Engle shrugged his shoulders. "Yeah, you know baseball. So what?"

Dugan added, "What's that got to do with Hilton?"

"Everything. He's a cinch to make the big leagues. He can't miss."

"Why can't he miss?" Dugan asked.

"Well, for one thing, he throws a lightning fast fastball. And, unlike a lot of chuckers, he's got marvelous control."

"What makes you think he won't burn himself out?" Engle asked.

"Because he's got that lanky, rawboned build most of the great pitchers have. Besides, he's six-four, 185 pounds, and he's got big hands."

"There's a lot of guys on the squad like that," Dugan protested. "Rickard and Dean and—"

"Sure," Wilder agreed, "but none of them are as fast or as well coordinated. You saw him play football and basketball, didn't you? No, Chip Hilton is a natural. He'll go straight to the top, right to a big-league team."

"So he makes the big leagues. Where do you come in?" Dugan asked.

"I'm going to get him connected," Wilder said calmly.

"Get him connected?" Dugan repeated weakly. "You mean now? Before he graduates?"

"That's right."

"What would that get *you?*" Engle asked.

"Plenty," Wilder said mysteriously. "I've got an agreement with somebody who's big in baseball. He used to play in the majors. If I can get Hilton to play ball with this guy, I'll get a finder's fee."

Dugan was bewildered. He looked at Wilder and shook his head. "You're crazy. Wouldn't that make him a professional? Or you even?"

Wilder grinned. "Maybe yes and maybe no," he said evasively. "Anyway, I'm starting my little campaign right now. Tonight! I'll see you later."

Chip was happy to take advantage of the short practice session. It gave him a chance to put in a little extra time on his job at Grayson's. George Grayson, his employer, was a real sports fan and very proud of the fact that three of his part-time workers were candidates for the team. Grayson was a good man and popular in the town of University, and the State students who worked for him greatly respected him. But the after-school absence of the three ballplayers placed an extra load on the other members of the staff, and Chip, Soapy, and Fireball utilized every opportunity they had to make up for it. Chip was in charge of the stockroom, and Soapy and Fireball worked the old-fashioned soda counter in the food court.

All the tables and booths were filled, and the fountain was lined with customers when Chip arrived. The beautiful spring weather seemed perfect for an ice cream cone or one of Grayson's many sundae concoctions, and the college students and University residents were out in droves. Whitty Whittemore was so busy behind the counter that he didn't even see Chip head back to the stockroom. Chip changed into Soapy's serving uniform—white slacks and a red-and-blue polo shirt—and hustled out to the fountain.

"Thanks, Chip! Am I ever glad to see you!" Whitty said.

"I can help out until Soapy and Fireball get here," Chip said. "They should be along pretty soon."

But Soapy and Fireball didn't show up until six o'clock. By that time, the fountain rush was over. Chip was glad to surrender Soapy's uniform and get back to his own job in the stockroom.

A few minutes after Chip left the deserted fountain, Widow Wilder sidled up to the counter and ordered a milk shake. Whitty and Fireball were talking at the other end of the fountain, and Soapy took the order. While Soapy was serving the talkative catcher, Wilder surprised the redhead with a big smile.

"You and Hilton stood us on our heads this afternoon, Smith. Nice goin'!"

"Er, thanks, Wilder," Soapy said awkwardly. "Chip did it."

"You did your part," the big athlete said smoothly. "The pitcher is only half of the battery, you know."

Soapy shook his head. "Maybe. Anyway, you and Hex weren't exactly fooling around. Hex struck me out twice in a row. He's a great pitcher."

"He's good," Wilder acknowledged, "but you were catching a greater one. I don't suppose I'm telling you anything you don't know, but—" Wilder slickly paused, then continued dramatically, "I think Chip Hilton is the best college pitcher in the country. Bar none!"

"It's great of you to say that—" Soapy began.

"I mean it! Man, I've been hanging around major-league baseball players all my life. I know a major-leaguer when I see one—and I saw one this afternoon. He's a ballplayer's player."

Soapy was beaming. "You're so right," he said. "Chip would like to know you said that."

Wilder shook his head. "Uh-uh, Smith. This little conversation was strictly between you and me. Well, see you around."

Soapy watched the burly catcher swagger over to the cashier's desk and pay Mitzi Savrill and walk out the door. Soapy's gaze never wavered until Wilder disappeared into the crowd and crossed the street. Even then, Soapy continued to peer out the window.

Soapy's behavior was so unusual that Fireball and Whitty exchanged glances. Never before, in their memory, had Soapy Smith failed to concentrate on Mitzi Savrill when his glance got that far.

"He must be sick," Fireball said.

"It's gotta be serious," Whitty agreed. "Did he get beaned this afternoon?"

Fireball shook his head and tapped Soapy on the shoulder. "What's the matter, Soapy? What's with you and Wilder?"

Soapy whirled around, grinning happily. "What a guy!" he said. "What a guy!"

"Why?" Whitty demanded.

"You should've heard what he said about Chip. He said Chip was the best college pitcher in the country. How about that!"

"That's no news," Fireball said.

"Coming from *him* it's news," Soapy said. "He's majors' material himself. He knows more about baseball than anyone around."

Fireball snorted and then commented shortly, "What makes you think he's an authority?"

A BALLPLAYER'S PLAYER

"Well, I saw him catch the varsity games last year, and I know he plays a lot of summer ball, and he knows a lot of the major-league players, and . . . Well, isn't that enough?"

"Not enough to make him a major-leaguer," Whitty said.

"Makes him a big-leaguer in my book," Soapy retorted stubbornly.

Fireball and Whittemore made sure Soapy got plenty of big-league talk the rest of the evening. Their customers were bewildered by the references to famous baseball stars Whittemore and Finley professed to know.

Soapy was glad when the evening was over and he and Chip reached their room in Jeff. They were both tired and wasted little time getting ready for bed. Before turning out the light, Soapy peered out the window. "Lots of stars in the sky, Chip. That means we work outside again tomorrow afternoon."

"Sounds good to me," Chip murmured sleepily. He was half-asleep when Soapy suddenly sat up in bed and turned on his reading light.

"You know something?" Soapy said. "I like Widow Wilder."

Chip raised himself up on his elbows and regarded the redhead. "What brought that on?"

"Something he said about you tonight at Grayson's."

"What?"

"He said you're a cinch to make the big leagues."

"Forget that kind of stuff, Soapy."

"But that's what he said," Soapy protested. "And he ought to know."

"Why?"

"Because he was the varsity catcher last year."

"What's that got to do with me?"

"Well, he's experienced. He knows a real ballplayer when he sees one. Not that *I* don't know you're good enough for the majors, but—"

"But what?"

"Well, I'm just an ordinary catcher. I'll be lucky if I get to warm up the bullpen pitchers."

"You mean you're giving up? Just like that?" Chip demanded.

"Chip, you know what I mean."

"No, I don't," Chip said shortly. "Now let's get some sleep. Saturday mornings are tough in the stockroom."

Soapy nodded. "Yeah, and we gotta be in good shape for practice in the afternoon. Maybe Coach Bennett will have another practice game. G'night."

Chip was right about the Saturday morning rush. The sun was warm and bright, and it brought everyone downtown in droves. Grayson's was jammed almost as soon as the doors opened, and every department was rushed. Chip had eaten a light breakfast and was half-starved by twelve o'clock. But he forgot all about eating when Soapy trotted in with a copy of the *News*. "Look!" Soapy exclaimed, shoving the paper into Chip's hands. "Coach Bennett! He's in the hospital; he's gotta have an operation!"

The story was right on the front page, and Chip concentrated on the bad news without comment. But not Soapy. He leaned over Chip's shoulder and kept up a running commentary: "'State coach in hospital! Del Bennett, State's head baseball coach, stricken with gallbladder attack. Immediate operation necessary.'"

"It's too bad," Chip said slowly.

"The paper says he had the attack right after practice," Soapy continued. "Dr. Terring made the diagnosis. Hey! Wonder if Rock knows about it?"

A BALLPLAYER'S PLAYER

"I'm sure he does, Soapy. Look, I've got to get busy if I'm going to get out of here in time for practice."

"Me too," Soapy called, dashing for the door.

A lot of people were talking about Coach Del Bennett that morning. And, as far as the State baseball team was concerned, perhaps the three people most concerned were discussing the sudden blow at that precise moment in State's athletic office.

Dad Young, State's athletic director, was seated behind his desk and talking to Henry Rockwell and Jim Corrigan.

"Hank," Young stated decisively, "you'll have to take charge. You can have Jim for your assistant until Del gets back."

"What about the freshmen?" Corrigan asked.

"Sullivan will take over," Young said.

"It's a tough break for Del," Rockwell said sympathetically. "We've got one of the greatest squads in the history of the school, and he's sick."

"Tough break for you too," Corrigan said quietly.

"What do you mean?" Rockwell asked.

"I mean you'd better win. Everybody is bragging about this year's team. You lose and you'll have all the wolves in the state on your neck."

"*Our* necks," Rockwell pointedly corrected.

Dad Young laughed. "I'm not worried. You'll do all right. Do you want me to come down to the field and talk to the players?"

"I wish you would," Rockwell said. "Come on, Jim, we'd better make some plans. Want to join us for lunch, Dad?"

"No, you men go ahead. I'll see you at 2:30 in front of the bleachers."

Following lunch, the two coaches got down to business. Rockwell wrote the names of the players on a piece of paper, and he and Corrigan then discussed the potential of each player.

"They all look good," Corrigan said shortly. "That's the trouble."

"Lots of players look good in practice, Jim," Rockwell said gently. "But you can tell a real ballplayer only by checking him like the major-league scouts do—"

"You mean in action?"

"That's right."

Corrigan nodded. "I'll go along with that."

"Yes," Rockwell continued thoughtfully, "you have to watch a player under fire, in action, when the chips are down. Not once, but time after time. You have to watch him in game after game and in situation after situation, noting his reactions, decisions, and performance in plays that call for split-second timing, poise, and confidence."

"That's fine when you have time, Rock," Corrigan said, "but we've got only two weeks, remember?"

"We could do the next best thing," Rockwell mused. "We could play some squad games."

"Right!" Corrigan agreed enthusiastically. "That'll work." He thought about it a second and then shook his head doubtfully. "Or will it? We're sitting on a powder keg now."

"What do you mean?"

"You know, the cliques. The factions on the team— Wilder and his bunch, Hex and the seniors, and, well, you know the others."

Rockwell nodded. "Yes, I know the others. You mean my Valley Falls kids, right?"

Corrigan smiled apologetically. "Well, I guess you can't blame them. It's a matter of self-protection, more or less."

"They're no better than the rest, Jim. It's our job to wreck the cliques before they wreck the ball club."

Choosing Sides

CHIP, SOAPY, AND FIREBALL were late, and the locker room was empty except for Murph Kelly. "Better get a move on," the trainer growled. "Dad Young is going to talk to the team about Del Bennett. Going to put your old coach in charge, Chip."

"You sure?" Soapy asked.

"Sure I'm sure," Kelly said. "Who else? Good man."

"You're telling us," Soapy said, nodding his head aggressively. "Rock won twenty-six state baseball championships in thirty-five years while he was at Valley Falls. And—"

"Come on, Soapy," Chip said impatiently. "Murph knows all about the Rock."

Dad Young had finished his talk and was heading back toward the field house when Chip, Soapy, and Fireball reached the bleachers. They sat down in the back row just as Rockwell began to talk.

"Men, Coach Corrigan and I are just as sorry as you are that Coach Bennett can't be with us. We'll try to carry on until he gets back; perhaps we can speed his recovery by getting in good shape and winning a couple of games for him.

"The first game is just two weeks away, two weeks from today. The best way to get a line on a ballplayer is to see him in action. So we're going to stage a five-game intrasquad series starting Monday afternoon. Hex, you and Wilder will act as squad captains and choose the players you want on your teams. Right now. Step out here with me and think it over. Jim, you toss a coin. Your call, Hex."

Corrigan tossed a coin in the air, and Rickard called "Heads!"

"It's tails," Corrigan said, picking up the coin. "Your choice, Wilder."

Wilder grinned and moved out in front of the bleachers. He stood there for a second and then pivoted quickly and pointed toward Chip. "Hilton!" he announced dramatically.

"Over there beside Wilder, Chip," Rockwell said softly.

It was Hex Rickard's turn now, and every eye was on him as he pondered his selection. "He'll choose a catcher," Chip breathed.

Hex took a long time to make his decision. "Cohen," he said at last.

Chip agreed with that call. Biggie was the best ballplayer on the field.

"Soapy Smith!" Wilder said clearly. This time the buzz of surprise was clearly audible.

Chip couldn't figure it out. Why was Wilder choosing him and Soapy ahead of Al Engle, Dugan, Reed, and the Harris brothers?

Rickard was surprised too. He hesitated briefly and

CHOOSING SIDES

then chose a catcher, Al Engle. Wilder chose Lee Carter, and the selections continued until every player in the bleachers had been chosen.

When the two captains had finished selecting their teams, Rockwell sent the players through the regular practice program and then dismissed them with the warning that they would have time for only a brief warm-up before the scrimmage game Monday afternoon.

"Rickard, Wilder, you men will have complete control of your lineups and substitutions. Jim and I are going to take notes," he said, "from the bleachers."

As soon as Rockwell excused them, the players formed into the usual groups and started for the locker room. Chip and his friends led the way, in a hurry to get to work. Behind them, How Rickard and his buddies tagged along slowly. Still farther behind, Widow Wilder, Al Engle, Doogie Dugan, George Reed, Lee Carter, and the two Harris brothers followed. Doogie Dugan was talking loudly.

"What's the big idea, Widow?" Dugan griped bitterly. "Why Hilton?"

"And why Soapy Smith?" Engle added.

"You know why," Wilder countered easily. "I told you yesterday."

"You didn't say anything about Smith," Engle said angrily. "Why pick him?"

"Take it easy," Wilder said calmly. "These games don't mean anything."

"Not to *you,* maybe," Dugan said sullenly, "but they mean a lot to us. We're new here. We've *got* to look good and show the coaches what we can do."

"You will," Wilder said. "Now listen. Al is the only catcher Rickard has, right? That means he catches all the games. I've got Smith *and* Nickels. That means I can control both of them. I certainly don't expect to ride the bench, so they aren't going to do much receiving."

"How about the pitching?" Dugan asked.

"Well, what about it?" Wilder retorted. "You heard what Rockwell said—I run the team. You'll get plenty of work."

"OK." Dugan shrugged grudgingly. "But I still don't understand it."

"You will. Wait and see."

Chip, Soapy, and Fireball dressed quickly and took off for Grayson's. On the way, they talked over the selections for the first time.

"So what do you think of Wilder now?" Soapy demanded.

"What do you mean?" Finley asked.

"Didn't I tell you he was a great guy?"

Fireball laughed. "You mean you think he's a great guy because he picked you for his team? What does that make *me*? And what about Biggie and Red and Diz Dean and—"

"But he picked Chip and me *before* he picked Dugan and Engle. Doesn't that mean anything?"

"It means *something*," Chip said thoughtfully.

"Well, here we are," Soapy announced, grinning. "Good old Grayson's, the best college meeting place in town!"

"And look at all those people around the fountain." Fireball groaned. "Wonder what the people in this town would do if burgers and ice cream were outlawed? C'mon, Soapy. Whitty must be going crazy."

Chip was kept as busy as Soapy, Fireball, and Whitty. His job involved inputting the inventory on the computer, filling department orders, and running downstairs and upstairs and in and out of the stockroom all evening. When he and Soapy headed for home, they were too tired even to talk baseball. They piled into their beds mumbling no more than a sleepy "good night."

The next morning, Soapy, as usual, was the first one up, and he ran downstairs to Jeff's big front porch to grab the newspapers from the stacks that were delivered every day to the dorm. When he returned, he and Chip buried their noses in the sports pages.

The *News* and the *Herald* each carried a number of State sports stories: Del Bennett's operation, the appointment of Henry Rockwell as acting head coach, and, of course, State's great baseball prospects.

There was one small story, too, about Pacifica College coming under investigation for NCAA violations. "Listen to this, Chip!" Soapy said excitedly. "This player supposedly accepted money for playing in a summer league. Seems this kid did it for a couple of years." Soapy looked blankly at Chip. "I don't get it. What's it all about?"

"You know the NCAA rules, Soapy. If this guy signed a contract—or even if he didn't sign anything but got paid for playing—he's a professional. He jeopardizes his school's eligibility for conference or national championships as well as his own eligibility to play. It's serious, Soapy."

"No decent guy would do that," Soapy commented.

"That's for sure," Chip agreed.

Without warning, the door crashed open and Speed Morris, Biggie Cohen, Red Schwartz, and Fireball Finley piled into the room. "Save me, Chip! Help me, Soapy," Speed yelled. "I need help! These deserters have me surrounded."

"Deserters!" Finley echoed. "You're the deserter! We're on the varsity. We're on Hex Rickard's team."

"So that's it," Soapy said, breaking into the argument. "Well, you guys have a surprise coming. Mr. Widow Wilder's team has all the brains. Wilder knows more baseball than Rickard will *ever* know."

"Not so!" Finley said succinctly.

"We've been figuring out the lineups, Chip," Biggie said. "We've got ours all set. How about your team?"

"Let's hear your lineup first," Soapy interrupted. "Then we'll let you help us make our championship batting order, right, Chip?"

"Right," Chip said. "Go ahead, Biggie."

Biggie smiled, winked at Soapy, and then shrugged his massive shoulders. "OK. Well, we think Hex will lead off with Russ Merton at shortstop; 'Minnie' Minson at third base as the push-along guy; 'Belter' Burke in left field and hitting third; Fireball in—"

"*You've* always batted in the cleanup position," Fireball objected.

"Well, then," Biggie continued, "I'll hit fourth and play first base. Fireball will be in center field, batting fifth. Red—or Bill Bentley—will be in right field, hitting sixth. 'Tubby' Ryder, playing second base and batting seventh. Al Engle will catch—he's our only catcher—and bat eighth, and Hex, naturally, will pitch."

"Right, and we've got Diz Dean and Terrell Sparks for pitchers to help Hex," Fireball added. "Let's have a look at your scrub lineup."

Soapy struck a fighting pose. "Scrub lineup? With *me* catching?"

Fireball laughed quietly. "Like you'll have a chance to do any catching on Widow Wilder's team! Why do you think he picked you?"

"Well, why didn't he pick Al Engle?" Soapy retorted.

"That's easy," Fireball said mockingly, shaking his

head. "He wanted to make sure he and Al Engle did *all* the catching. For *both* teams."

"I don't believe it," Soapy said stubbornly.

"All right, all right," Biggie interrupted. "Let's have your lineup."

"Go ahead, Chip," Speed urged. "You set it up."

"Well," Chip said thoughtfully, "I think Wilder will use Ozzie Crowell at second base and as his leadoff man; Speed at shortstop and in the bunt position; Reggie Harris at first base and in the number-three hitting slot; Murphy Gillen in right field and in the big-hitter spot; George Reed in center field and as the fifth batter; Lee Carter in left field, hitting sixth; Andre Durley on third base and as the seventh hitter, and either Soapy or Widow himself as the catcher."

"Well," Red Schwartz urged, "go on. Who's working the mound?"

"They've only got one pitcher," Fireball interrupted. "Chip!"

"What about Dugan and Harris?" Chip remonstrated.

"Who are you trying to kid, Chip?" Biggie said, draping a huge arm around Chip's shoulder. "Don't be modest with us. We've tried to hit that marble you throw at the plate, remember?"

"I wish that were true," Chip said lightly. "Whoa! Look at the time. I've got to get to church. See you guys later."

Chip attended services and then decided to take a walk to limber up. He stepped out the door briskly and headed for the campus lake below the football stadium. It was a beautiful day, and Chip's spirits soared. It didn't seem possible that he was a sophomore at State and likely to be a varsity pitcher. He was doing all right in his classes too. That was the big thing. And he was president of Jeff, vice president of the sophomore class, and also working while attending college.

Chip began to think about his mom in Valley Falls and his job at Grayson's; about George Grayson, his generous employer; Mitzi Savrill, the store's cashier and the love of Soapy's life; the fountain crew, Soapy and Fireball and Whitty Whittemore; and last but not least, his stockroom assistant, young Isaiah Redding.

"I'm lucky," Chip said aloud, unaware that he had voiced the thought. "Really lucky."

"Who's lucky?" a voice boomed behind him.

Chip, startled, pivoted to face Widow Wilder and a man he had never seen before. The man with Wilder looked like an athlete. He had wide shoulders, a strong bull-like neck, and a deep tan. The stranger's hair was gray, and there were little sun wrinkles extending out from the corners of his dark eyes.

"This is Jon Hart, Chip," Wilder said eagerly. "He's my summer boss. Jon, this is Chip Hilton."

"Glad to meet you, Hilton," the man said, smiling and extending his hand in a firm clasp.

"Wilder has been telling me a lot about you. In fact, that's why I'm here. In addition to my other contacts in baseball, I work for a fishing outfit in Alaska and manage their company team. I'd like you to come up and do a little pitching for us this summer."

"You'll like it there, Chip," Wilder said quickly. "Mr. Hart has lots of connections and helps players get noticed by the big leagues."

Chip smiled. "But I have a summer job at a summer camp: Camp All-America in New York State."

"We'll give you a better job," Hart said convincingly.

"Yeah, and you can play baseball all summer," Wilder added. "You can't do that in a camp job."

CHOOSING SIDES

"What kind of work would I have to do?"

Hart laughed heartily. "Work?" he repeated. "A pitcher like you?" Then, noting Chip's serious expression, he continued quickly. "No, the men backing our teams make it pretty easy for our best employees to concentrate on playing ball."

"I'm not sure I understand you, sir. Are you saying I would mostly just be playing ball?"

"Mostly or exclusively if you're as good as Mitch here says you are."

"But wouldn't that make me a professional?"

"I don't see how it could. We're not playing in an organized league, you know. We play town ball. And," Hart said pointedly, "all I can say is that practically every player in our league is a college player. We wouldn't have any other kind."

"You'll have to count me out," Chip said. "I wouldn't take a chance on playing any sport if I thought it would make me ineligible for college ball. Thanks just the same."

"That's all right, Hilton," Hart said pleasantly. "If you change your mind, just tell Wilder. He'll know where to get in touch with me."

CHAPTER 4

Unscrupulous Men

STATE UNIVERSITY CAMPUS was buzzing with base-ball talk the next morning—in the classrooms, in the halls, and along the broad, shrubbery-lined walks connecting one building to the next. It seemed everybody was planning to be in the bleachers that afternoon to see the first game of the intrasquad series. And for the first time, Chip began to get that tight feeling in his chest, the old, familiar mixture of excitement, anxiety, and pressure.

Chip could almost feel the tension in the air when he walked into the locker room. Soapy, Biggie, Speed, Red, and Fireball greeted him with their usual friendliness, but there was a strange and unusual hoarseness in their voices. This was an important day for Chip and a lot of the players.

"Coach wants everyone in the field-house bleachers in ten minutes!" Murph Kelly shouted.

Chip dressed quickly and walked over to the field house with Fireball and his Valley Falls friends.

UNSCRUPULOUS MEN

"Wonder what it's all about," Soapy commented.

They soon found out. Murph Kelly was the last to reach the bleachers and nodded to Rockwell. "All set, Coach. They're all here."

Rockwell moved out in front of the bleachers and got right to the point. "Well, we've got a fine day to start off our series. I just wanted to clear up a few things for Coach Bennett before we get into our season. In light of the events unfolding at Pacifica College, I just want to remind you of some of the issues our NCAA compliance officer and Coach Bennett discussed with you."

Rockwell paused and paced slowly back and forth. In the short interim, Wilder, Engle, and Dugan moved their heads close together and exchanged whispers. Rockwell continued after a few seconds.

"Coach Bennett, Coach Corrigan and I are concerned about the situation involving a few unscrupulous men whose only interest in a player is to make a few dollars by offering him opportunities that will end up costing the athlete his college eligibility. As college men, it is assumed that your purpose in coming to college is to get an education, a degree, and prepare yourselves for the future.

"Now, Coach Bennett and I are fully aware that there are a number of players on this squad who are capable of playing organized ball, maybe even major league baseball. But a man can't have his cake and eat it too. If you sign any sort of an agreement with a baseball organization, you can't play college baseball. By the way, you'll find the NCAA eligibility rules posted on the bulletin board in the locker room. Take a look at them.

"Now let's get going. We'll take thirty minutes for hitting and fielding practice and then play a seven-inning game. By the way, we've arranged for a couple of umpires to run the games. Hex, you and Wilder take charge. And good luck. You won the toss, Wilder, so you get the home-team dugout and field first."

Chip was in a hurry to get into the warm sunlight and loosen up. He walked slowly along beside Soapy until they came to the home-team dugout. Wilder had preceded them and turned to toss a ball to Soapy. "You warm up Doogie and Chip, Smith. I want to get my lineup set." He tossed another ball to Lenny Harris. "Throw to the hitters, Lenny, OK? Nickels, you catch."

Soapy walked quickly to the practice plate and waited for Chip and Dugan. Dugan accompanied Chip to the warm-up rubber. Soapy tossed the ball to Doogie, and the sullen pitcher took the first throw. Then Chip and Dugan alternated their throws. Neither said a word. Dugan's obvious antagonism was enough to drive Chip into a shell as he concentrated on his control.

Wilder's players began to take their hits, and over on the other side of the field, Hex Rickard's players were busy with a pepper-ball game. Between throws, Chip checked the batting order that Wilder was supervising at the plate. It was the same he had selected, except for the battery. "It's Dugan and Nickels," he muttered.

But Chip was wrong. Wilder turned and waved his arm. "Get your licks now, Chip. You too, Smith. You guys are starting the game."

Soapy let out a whoop, dropped his glove, and ran for the bat rack. Doogie Dugan mumbled something, threw his glove to the ground, and stomped down into the dugout. Soapy grabbed a bat and winked at Chip. "What do you know!" he said significantly.

Chip didn't know anything and didn't care much about anything except that he was going to pitch. When Soapy laid down his bunt and ran it out, Chip stepped up to the plate. He met the first two pitches easily and then took a full cut. The ball went out on a line nearly to the fence, and Chip grunted in satisfaction. Good! Then he laid one down, ran it out, and went back to the warm-up rubber.

Rickard and his team started their hitting then, and Wilder called his team together in front of the dugout. "Here's the way we'll hit," he said. "Crowell, Morris, Harris, Gillen, Reed, Carter, Durley, Smith, and Hilton. Nickels, you hit to the outfield. I'll take the infield warm-up."

He turned to Lenny Harris. "Lenny, you take the first-base coaching box when the game starts. I'll cover third base. Chip, you'd better throw a few more."

Soapy picked up his glove, and the two friends resumed their warm-up throws. A few minutes later, the umpire called, "Play ball," and Chip walked out to the mound.

While Chip waited for Soapy to get on his catching gear, he tossed a ball back and forth with Speed and looked around at his teammates. Reggie Harris was on first base, Ozzie "The Whiz" Crowell was at the keystone-sack position, Andre Durley was at third base, and Speed was at short. It was a good infield. Speed, Crowell and Durley were all sophomores and had played together as freshman teammates.

Sophomore Murphy Gillen was in right field; George Reed, a senior, was in center field, with Lee Carter, a junior, in left field. With his buddy Soapy behind the plate, what more could Chip want?

Chip turned toward the plate and studied Russ Merton. Russ was a senior and veteran leadoff man. At five-seven and weighing 150 pounds, he was all ballplayer. Russ had a keen eye and the reputation for waiting the pitchers out.

PAY-OFF PITCH

Soapy gave the sign, and Chip stepped forward to toe the rubber. He stretched, lowered his arm, and shot his fastball down and out and across the plate, knee-high, for a called strike.

"That's the way to start a ball game," Chip breathed as he took Soapy's return peg. He turned and walked behind the mound again and waited for Soapy's sign. This time he took a full stretch, waited, gathered his weight, and dealt. The ball sailed inside and low, but the umpire called it a strike.

"Lucky," Chip muttered.

"Way out in front, Chipper," Soapy cried. "Let's get the big one."

Merton waited until Chip got the sign and toed the rubber and then dropped back out of the batter's box. He gave the umpire a long look while Soapy protested the delay. When he stepped back into the box, Chip bore down, and his fastball sizzled across Merton's knees. Russ's swing was late. The ball thumped into Soapy's glove, and the redhead had fired it down the first-base line to Reggie Harris before the little shortstop regained his balance. One down!

"Simple, isn't it?" Soapy yelled. "Well, let's carry on. Who's next?"

Jaime "Minnie" Minson was next. He tossed away a spare bat, knocked the dirt out of his spikes with the remaining bat, pulled his batting helmet down over his eyes, and stepped into the box. Minson was a five-ten, 185-pound veteran who played the hot corner like a pro. The stocky fighter could hit anything with stitches.

"Come on, Chipper," Soapy yelled. "One is good, but two is gooder!"

Chip came in low with another fast one that Minson

looked over carefully and let go by. It was close, but the umpire called it a ball.

"Evens up," Chip muttered.

He twisted one across the outside corner for a called strike, drove one inside around the wrists for another ball, and then came back with a tight curve that cut across the outside corner. Minson reached and got a piece of it, and the ball came back to Chip on a big hop. It was an easy out. Two away!

"Pepper ball!" Soapy shouted gleefully. "Come on, Chip. Let the rest of the guys get in the game."

Ellis "Belter" Burke was next, and Chip knew all about him. A player didn't dare give the big left fielder anything around or above the waist. Belter's nickname was for real! He was a pull hitter, and when he got hold of one, he powered it out of sight.

"Three up and three down, Chip. That's the way, baby! Throw that apple in here, babe!"

Chip took Soapy's sign and whipped in a fast one, low and outside. It hit the corner for a called strike. His next pitch was an inside change-up just below the belt. Burke stepped into it, fouling the ball off the handle for strike two.

"Way ahead, Chipper. Way ahead! Give it to me, baby!"

Chip put his back into the next throw, zipping it across the corner, low and inside. Burke tried to golf it out of the ballpark, but he missed the ball by a mile, spun around, and nearly fell. Soapy was halfway to the dugout before Belter recovered his balance.

Rickard set Crowell, Morris, and Harris down, one-two-three, and it seemed to Chip that he had hardly gotten his warm-up jacket on before it was time to take it off again.

PAY-OFF PITCH

Biggie led off in the top of the second and got hold of one of Chip's fastballs. But he was a little too far under the ball, and Murphy Gillen pulled it down from the fence. Fireball drove a hard roller straight at Speed and was an easy out at first. Bentley struck out on three fast ones around the knees.

Chip and Hex both had their stuff and maintained the pace for five innings. Chip had eight strikeouts and Hex had four. It was fine pitching. The score: Wilder 0, Rickard 0. Both teams made changes for the sixth inning. Wilder took Soapy's place, sent Chip to right field in place of Murphy Gillen, put Doogie Dugan on the mound, and sent Lenny Harris and Darrin Nickels to the outfield in place of Carter and Reed. Rickard took himself out of the game and put Diz Dean on the mound. Then he sent Red Schwartz, Ned Diston, and Terrell Sparks to the outfield.

Doogie Dugan, who was now pitching for Wilder's squad, immediately got into trouble. He walked Bill Bentley, hit Ted Ryder with a pitched ball, and then, trying too hard to strike out Al Engle, threw one into the dirt.

The ball got away from Wilder, which moved Bentley and Ryder to third and second. Engle caught the next pitch on the nose for a three-bagger, and Rickard's team led, 2-0. Diz Dean struck out, Russ Merton beat out a bunt, and Red Schwartz, batting in Burke's place, hit into a double play.

Wilder's team came to bat in the bottom of the sixth, behind but anxious to improve. Reggie Harris was first up to bat and got hold of one of Dean's fastballs. It looked like a sure three-bagger, but Red Schwartz pulled it in on a dead run for the initial out. Nickels struck out, and George Reed grounded out to Biggie Cohen. The score at the end of six innings: Wilder 0, Rickard 2.

UNSCRUPULOUS MEN

Dugan got by in the top of the seventh on the strength of some superb infield play by Crowell, Speed Morris, and Andre Durley, and Wilder's team came to bat in the bottom of the seventh with Andre up, Widow on deck, and Chip in the hole. It was now or never!

Andre Durley stood five feet, six inches in his stocking feet. And when he crouched at the plate, he squeezed the strike zone down to zero. Diz Dean tried to hold back his speed, but he couldn't find the plate as a result. So Andre gained his base on balls, and then Wilder was up with a chance to tie the game.

Dean made another mistake. He tried to fire his fastball past the bulky catcher. But Wilder liked the pitches fast! He caught a two-and-two pitch squarely on the nose. The ball screamed its way out through middle right and clear to the fence. Durley scored, but Red Schwartz fired the ball back to the infield in time to hold Wilder at third base. That brought Chip to bat with a chance to win the game.

CHAPTER 5

Number-One Pitcher

FASTBALL PITCHERS are most effective when they keep the hitters off balance. Most speedball artists keep the batters guessing with their change of pace. But not Diz Dean. The big lefty's blazing pitches were as wild as they were fast. Control? Diz's pitches were just as likely to dart toward a batter's head, as they were to zip over the plate.

Chip batted from either side and liked fastball pitching. Hex Rickard thought about that while Chip was advancing toward the plate; then he made a sudden decision. He called Terrell "Flash" Sparks, a curveball pitcher, in from the outfield and sent Dean to the outfield in his place.

While Sparks was taking his warm-up pitches, Chip walked around behind Engle to the first-base side of the plate and waited patiently for Sparks to finish his throws. When Chip stepped up to the plate, Engle opened up.

NUMBER-ONE PITCHER

"Big star now hitting, Flash. Throw it where he can hit it. Gotta keep him happy, you know."

Sparks's first pitch was a soft curve that broke across Chip's knees. Chip let it go for a called strike. Behind him, he could hear Soapy, Speed, Durley, and Crowell yelling, "Get hold of one, Chip!" and "Let 'er rip, Chipper!"

Sparks's next pitch was on the outside and waist-high, and Chip went for it. There was a sharp crack! The ball took off on a line for the top of the right-field fence. It looked like a certain home run, but it was a line smash and just didn't have the height. The ball cracked against the fence about a foot below the top before bouncing back toward center field.

Chip sprinted around first and second and was figuring on stretching the hit into a home run. But Diz Dean played the ball just right, backing up toward center field and taking the ball on the rebound. Then he fired a long, one-bounce throw all the way to the plate. Chip rounded third base and then saw the ball coming in to Engle on a perfect line.

"Can't make it," Chip grunted, pulling up. Just then, he saw Engle send a throw to third. Chip barely got back to the bag, just ahead of the ball.

Wilder tallied to tie up the score at two all, and then Ozzie Crowell was up. "The Whiz" batted lefty and on the second pitch laid down a perfect squeeze bunt. Chip was in and across the plate with the winning run before Sparks fielded the ball. The final score: Wilder 3, Rickard 2.

Wilder was waiting when Chip scored and grabbed him by the arm. "That's the way, Chip!" he said. "I *knew* you could do it. That's why I put you in the outfield."

Speed, Biggie, Red, Fireball, and Soapy surrounded Chip, and then he and his five buddies walked slowly toward the field house. Chip was glad to get away from the big catcher.

But it wasn't that easy. That evening, when he took a break from work to get a sandwich at Pete's Place, Wilder was talking to Pete Thorpe, the owner of the restaurant and Chip's friend.

"Here he is now," Wilder said.

"Hi ya, Chip," Pete said warmly. "Widow has been telling me how you won your own game this afternoon."

"I didn't win it," Chip said quickly. "Ozzie Crowell squeezed in the winning run."

"So what!" Wilder said. "Your three-bagger tied up the score, and your run put us out in front." He turned to Pete. "You should've seen him. Eight strikeouts in five innings. How about serving us in the booth, Pete?"

"I've only got a couple of minutes, Wilder," Chip said quickly. "I've got to go right back to work."

Wilder wasn't going to be put off. He picked up his sandwich and ushered Chip to a booth. "There," he said. "Now we can talk for a few minutes. By the way, have you thought any more about this summer?"

Chip nodded. "I've thought about it a lot. It doesn't ring right to me."

"What do you mean?"

"I think it would make me a professional. Mr. Hart himself implied I would pretty much be getting paid to play ball. That's against all amateur rules."

"But we have jobs. Look! Just because our bosses let us off to play ball doesn't make us pros. Come on, Chip! I wasn't the only college player in the league. Why, there must have been five or six college players on some teams. Of course, some of the guys played under different names."

"That *proves* it's wrong."

"Why?"

"Why? Because they didn't play using their own names. If there wasn't something wrong with it, why didn't they use their own names?"

"I guess they could if they wanted to. I don't know all the answers, Chip. Last summer was my first year in the league, but I wouldn't have missed it for the world. Lots of the managers have connections with major-league scouts."

Wilder cleared his throat and continued self-importantly. "I met a couple myself."

"It's not for me."

"You're a chump. You'd burn up the league!"

"Not me, Wilder."

"Listen! My boss sends me some money every month. I bet you'd have to work day and night at Grayson's to make as much as I'm getting. I get it for free. Besides, I've been promised a big bonus the day I graduate. That is, if I stick it out that long. Man," Wilder exclaimed, shaking his head, "that bonus is looking bigger every day."

"But you can't take a bonus now. Not while you're playing college ball. Major-league teams won't let you play professional ball while you're in school. They know the rules."

"But I could go to the Caribbean or South America. Right now!"

"What about college?" Chip asked, leaning across the table to look directly into Mitch Wilder's dark eyes. "What about earning your degree?"

"What about it?" Wilder shrugged.

"You've only got one more year to go. One more year and you can graduate. Then, if something goes wrong in baseball, you can teach and coach or go into business or do most anything."

PAY-OFF PITCH

"You don't need a college diploma to go into business."

"I'm not sure you're right about that, Mitch. It helps to get a good start."

"Could be," Wilder said noncommittally. "Well, see you tomorrow. I'm going to start Harris in the Wednesday game and let Doogie finish it up. That way you'll be all set for Friday. I'm counting on you to win three games."

After Wilder left, Pete Thorpe came over to the booth. "Friend of yours?" he asked.

"Well, I guess so—"

"Sure talks a lot," Pete ventured. "He comes in here pretty regular lately. Always talking baseball and bragging about all the big-league players he knows. Guess he's a pretty good catcher though."

"He is, Pete. He's a good hitter too."

The restaurant door banged open, and Pete threw up his hands in mock terror. "Oh, oh!" he cried. "Here comes the human satellite."

Soapy rushed in excitedly. "Hi ya, Pete! Hi ya, Chip. Just met Wilder. Said you were here. Man! He thinks you're the greatest. Said he wished you could pitch *every* game. What a great guy! Said he was going to start you again on Friday and wanted to know if it would be all right with me if he did the receiving. Imagine that! Asking me!"

Soapy shook his head in wonder, his eyes wide and his cheeks all pink as if he had been in a fierce wind or the sun too long. "Wilder said he'd never seen *anyone* throw a ball so fast! What do you think about that?"

Chip laughed. "He was kidding you."

"No, he wasn't. He meant every word."

"I doubt it. Well, I've got to get back to the storeroom. See you later."

NUMBER-ONE PITCHER

After work Chip and Soapy walked home at a fast pace. They liked the walk up Main Street and across campus after work. It was a little longer than the usual student shortcut, but it was a more pleasant route for scenery, and it gave them a good chance to limber up and talk. When they got home, Soapy grabbed his *Abnormal Psychology* textbook and flopped down on his bed. Chip turned on his computer. Soapy looked up when he heard the familiar, "You've got mail!"

"Who's it from? Your mom?"

"Um, yes. There's one from my mom." Chip grinned sideways at Soapy.

"So, who else?"

"Well, there's some junk mail. Interested?"

"Nope, although I was hoping you had something from a secret admirer."

"Nothing doing." Chip laughed and pushed his best friend's comments away as he settled in to read his mom's message.

"Then I'll get back to my abnormal book," said Soapy.

Tuesdays and Thursdays were long days for Chip because of his science labs, and he was late that afternoon for practice. He dressed quickly and hurried out on the field. The players were working in small groups, and Chip joined the pitchers.

Later, he took part in the calisthenics and then warmed up for half an hour with Soapy. When it was his turn to hit, he found his timing perfect and met the ball surely and solidly. When he finished batting, he started toward the outfield to shag some flies. But Rockwell stopped him and ordered Chip and the rest of the pitchers to take five laps and hit the showers.

PAY-OFF PITCH

Hex Rickard fell in beside Chip as they trotted around the field, and when they completed the last lap, the two slowly walked together to the locker room.

"You really stood us on our heads yesterday, Chip," Rickard said, grinning amiably.

"You didn't do such a bad job yourself," Chip replied. "We were lucky."

Unnoticed, Doogie Dugan was right behind them. "Why all the bows, Hilton?" he said sarcastically. "I got credit for the win. We won while *I* was on the mound."

"I wasn't taking bows, Dugan," Chip said easily.

Dugan snorted. "Sure! Rockwell's had you taking bows for years."

"That's dumb."

"Oh, yeah? You know he's priming you for a big, fat baseball contract."

"That's not true!" Chip said hotly.

Dugan spit on the grass contemptuously. "We'll see. I know one thing for sure. You'll be pitching against all the soft touches."

"Cut it out, Dugan," Rickard remonstrated. "Quit being such a jerk. Where's your sportsmanship?"

Dugan turned on Rickard, venting his spite in a violent outburst. "He's got you fooled too, huh? Just like Wilder. Well, you'll find out. Wait and see who gets all the press. This ought to be your big year, but you'll see who gets the credit. You might've been State's numero-uno pitcher last year, but you haven't got a chance this year."

Rickard dropped back beside Dugan and placed a hand on his shoulder. "Look, Dugan, the team's the thing. None of us are looking for personal glory. You'd better forget about personalities and start thinking about the team." He slapped Dugan on the back. "Right now you need a cold shower."

Dugan jerked away and hurried on ahead. "You'll find out, Rickard," he said over his shoulder. "Don't say I didn't warn you."

Chip and Rickard continued along silently for a short distance. Then Rickard smiled and shrugged his shoulders. "Dugan doesn't know much about sportsmanship, does he, Chip?"

"He's just a little upset," Chip said gently.

CHAPTER 6

NCAA Notes

THE BLEACHERS filled up early Wednesday afternoon with students, professors, and fans from the town of University. The day was almost too good to be true; it was a warm, sunny afternoon, and everybody was in a baseball mood! Many of the people filling the bleachers in the spring sunshine had been big supporters of the previous year's freshman team, the Fence Busters. Others had followed the fortunes of the varsity. But the crowd was aware of the fierce competition the candidates were waging for starting positions on this year's varsity. And the fans were eager to defend their favorites.

Seated in the stands directly behind home plate were big Jim Collins, State's greatest baseball supporter, and his daughter Cindy, who was a sophomore at the college and Fireball Finley's biggest fan. Cindy watched her dad squirming in his seat and struggling to hold his tongue, trying not to join in on the baseball banter all around them.

"There can't be much question about the pitchers," one fan said loudly. "It's gotta be Rickard and Hilton."

"Of course!" someone said. "But which one is the number-one pitcher?"

Cindy knew it was coming minutes before her father opened his mouth. She recognized the signs—the squirming increased, accompanied now by a slight rocking motion; the arms folded and unfolded across his chest, and the tips of his ears and his neck turned red. She grinned to herself and watched him out of the corner of her eye as he poised himself for action. Finally he plunged right in, just as she had known he would.

"Hex and Chip are two of the finest pitchers in the State, but you can't beat Chip Hilton for his all-around athleticism!" Big Jim's voice boomed as he smiled and turned to address the fans behind him.

That really started something. Everybody in University knew Rickard was a great pitcher, and most of the fans knew Chip's reputation as the first State sophomore ever to be selected for the all-American football team. Naturally the basketball fans in the bleachers knew all about his accomplishments on the court too.

While the fans around Jim and Cindy were discussing Chip's and Hex's pitching merits, other fans in nearby sections were debating the players' abilities for other positions.

"Wilder is the only *real* catcher out there."

"How do you know? How do you know that big Nickels kid or Smith or that junior college catcher aren't as good?"

"You mean Engle? That carrot-top Smith did most of the catching for the freshman team last year. He's as good as Wilder any day!"

"No way! That freckle face hasn't got the experience," someone retorted.

"What do you think of that big guy on first base?"

"That's Biggie Cohen. He's a sophomore, right?" The girl wearing the State sweatshirt looked around for confirming nods.

"No one will beat that guy out," a large, athletic-looking guy stated.

"Cohen isn't the only sophomore who's good," the guy seated next to him added.

"I don't see how the coach can keep those two sophomore outfielders, Finley and Burke, out of the lineup either!"

"Who's the third outfielder?"

"Gotta be Bentley. He's a solid hitter, and he's had three years' experience. No one, but no one, can go farther and faster to pull in a fly ball."

"No argument there."

"I'm glad that's settled," someone gibed.

"Yeah," another chimed in. "Since you guys are doing the coaching this year, why don't you give us the rest of the infield starters?"

"Gotta go with the veterans there."

"Sure! Tubby Ryder and Russ Merton are the best double-play combination I ever saw in college ball."

"All right, how about third base?"

"Jaime Minson! No one is going to evict him from the hot corner."

"Well," someone said sarcastically, "you coaches better hurry up and decide on your lineups. The game is about to start."

Chip had warmed up and taken his batting practice with the rest of Wilder's players, but when the infield practice began, he walked back to the dugout and sat down beside Doogie Dugan. Dugan glared at him for a short moment and then picked up his glove and got to his feet. "This dugout isn't big enough for both of us," he said contemptuously as he walked away.

For the first time, Chip felt a sudden, blinding rage toward Doogie Dugan. He was on the verge of reaching out and smashing him back on the dugout bench. But Chip quickly reined in this emotion and sank back onto the bench, weak and sick at heart. *Why is Dugan so antagonistic?*

Rickard started Dean on the mound, and the big lefty was magnificent. His fastball was hopping, and, for once, he had no trouble with his control. Chip sat in the dugout and watched Dean mow down Crowell, Morris, and Harris in one-two-three order.

When Wilder's team took the field, Lenny Harris pitched with Darrin Nickels behind the plate. Harris had trouble from the first pitch. Russ Merton walked, Jaime Minson punched a perfect hit-and-run ball in the hole between first and second for a clean hit, and Ellis "Belter" Burke tripled to right-center. Merton and Minson scored.

Biggie Cohen, batting in the cleanup spot, looked over an outside pitch that the umpire called a ball and then pulled a letter-high fastball over the left-field fence for a home run. It was a tremendous hit that brought the crowd to its feet with a resounding cheer.

Harris walked Fireball. Then Bentley topped a low pitch, and he and Fireball were out in a beautiful double play, from Speed to Crowell to Harris. Ted Ryder struck out, and the inning ended with Rickard's team out in front, 4-0.

The first inning was a preview of the entire game. Mitch Wilder's team had trouble retiring Rickard's players in every inning, and Diz Dean had the burly catcher's hitters eating out of his hand. Wilder replaced Harris and Nickels with Doogie Dugan and Soapy in the sixth inning. But Rickard's hitters were in the groove and kept up their hitting. And as Rickard's hitters continued to bang the ball, Dugan grew increasingly upset. He acted like a little boy, challenging almost every call the plate umpire made against him. Soapy tried to help, but it was wasted on the angry pitcher.

Chip got in the game as a pinch hitter in the top of the ninth with George Reed and Lee Carter on second and third, and his double drove in the only two runs Wilder's team scored. Wilder didn't play. The final score: Richard 13, Wilder 2!

That tied up the series at one game each, and Rickard's players were jubilant, razzing Harris and Dugan all the way to the locker room. Harris took it with a good-natured grin, but Dugan could not handle it, and his sullen responses only made things worse for him. Rickard's players ragged the junior college pitcher even more because of his poor behavior.

Wilder caught up with Dugan and put his arm over the little pitcher's shoulder. "You'll get 'em the next time, Doogie. Don't worry about it. They had a hot hitting streak. Even Hilton couldn't have put out that fire."

That did it. Dugan jerked away from Wilder, his face flushed and his black eyes flashing angrily. "Hilton! It's always Hilton! What makes you think *he's* so great? What's he proved?"

Chip and Soapy, walking just ahead of Dugan and Wilder, couldn't help overhearing Doogie's outburst. Chip smiled ruefully, but Soapy didn't like it. "What's the matter with him, Chip?" Soapy growled. "He was doing the pitching. If he didn't like the signs, all he had to do was shake them off."

"I know, Soapy," Chip said gently. "Forget about it."

Forgetting about it was not so easy. Dugan was shaking with rage. He gestured ahead toward Chip and Soapy. "I can't pitch to Smith, Widow. Man, he's . . . he's just a high school catcher. A third-rate high school catcher!"

"You can't blame him for the hits, Doogie," Mitch Wilder responded calmly.

"He was calling 'em, wasn't he? Anyway, he doesn't know one pitch from another. How come *you* only want to catch when Hilton is pitching?"

"What are you talking about? I didn't catch when he pitched."

"But you said you were going to do the receiving on Friday, and he's going to pitch. How come you're using him twice in the first week?"

Wilder's face reddened. "That's my business," he said roughly. "I wouldn't talk about anyone else if I were you, Doogie. There's a lot of difference between a junior college pitcher and a major-leaguer."

Chip looked every inch a major-league player when he toed the rubber to deliver the first pitch of the game on Friday. Widow Wilder was behind the plate, looking as wide as a refrigerator, and Chip felt as loose as a noodle. His first pitch zipped across the plate for a called strike, and Widow Wilder whipped the ball back with a grunt of satisfaction. "All mine, big boy," he called. "Nothing to it."

There wasn't much to it. Wilder kept Chip on the mound for the full seven innings, and he was never in trouble. Hex Rickard went all the way for his team too. The game might well have ended in a scoreless game for both teams. But in the bottom of the sixth, with no one down, Wilder got ahold of one of Hex's fastballs. It flew through the infield and clear to the right-field fence. The big catcher held up at second.

PAY-OFF PITCH

Chip was up. He stepped into the batter's box on the third-base side of the plate to face Rickard's lefty pitching. Rickard came in with his fastball just below the belt, and Chip laid down a slow roller along the first-base line. The pitcher threw him out, but he advanced Wilder to third base. Ozzie Crowell, ever "The Whiz," then squeezed Wilder home for the only score of the game.

Chip breezed through Rickard's hitters in the top of the seventh, and the game was over. The score: Wilder 1, Rickard 0. That gave Wilder's team the lead in the series, two games to one.

The Saturday game was a complete reversal. Doogie Dugan and Soapy made up the battery for Wilder's team, and Rickard used Dean and Sparks. It was a free-hitting game, but Rickard's players had more power and won, 9-5. That evened the series at two games each. Monday's game would decide the series championship.

That evening at work, Chip was concentrating so much on Monday's game that he forgot all about the time. But hunger drove baseball out of his head around eight o'clock. He decided to get a quick sandwich.

"I'll be back in about twenty minutes, Isaiah," he told his high school stockroom assistant. "Call me at Pete's Place if you need me."

Pete's restaurant was only a few doors away on Tenth Street, and Chip mentally ran down Rickard's batting lineup as he walked along. "Whoa," he murmured to himself. "I'm acting as if Wilder *has* to start me."

Unexpectedly, Chip got the answer to his thoughts. As soon as he entered the restaurant, a familiar voice hailed him.

"Hey, Chip! Just talking about you. Over here in the booth. Come on, sit down. Bring him what he wants, Pete."

Chip turned. It was Wilder.

"Sure, Wilder, sure," Pete said. "Hi ya, Chip. You want the usual?"

Chip nodded and reluctantly walked over to the booth. He sat down across from Wilder. "I've been talking to myself about you," Chip said. "I was thinking about Monday's game."

"You should," Wilder said pointedly. "I was just telling Pete that you're going to win the championship for me on Monday. Here, look." He tossed a slip of paper over in front of Chip. "That's my batting order for the game."

Chip looked over Wilder's list: "Crowell, 2b; Morris, ss; Harris, 1b; Gillen, rf; Reed, cf; Carter, lf; Durley, 3b; Wilder, c; Hilton, p."

He looked up. Wilder was watching him intently.

"All right?" Wilder asked.

Chip nodded. "It sure is."

"We'll take them with you on the mound," Wilder said confidently. "You and me make up a major-league battery."

"That reminds me, Widow," Chip said, reaching into the pocket of his jeans and pulling out a folded piece of lined paper. "I made some notes from the NCAA manual. I didn't copy everything down, but I think I've got enough here for you to think about. Now, listen:

'An individual loses amateur status and thus shall not be eligible for intercollegiate competition in a particular sport if the individual a. uses his or her athletic skill (directly or indirectly) for pay in any form of that sport; b. accepts a promise of pay even if such pay is to be received following completion of intercollegiate athletics participation; c. signs a contract or commitment of any kind to play professional athletics; d. receives, directly or indirectly, a salary from a professional sports organization based upon athletic skill or participation.'"

Chip looked up from his notes and steadily eyed Mitch Wilder. "Well?"

Wilder shrugged. "I didn't sign a contract with a big-league team."

"How about the money you got for playing? And how about that assumed name you played under? If you didn't think what you were doing was wrong, why the phony name?" Chip countered.

"*I* didn't have anything to do with the name they put in the paper. The scorer did that, and I *had* a job. I had a right to get paid. Just like you do at Grayson's."

"But I *work* at Grayson's. You told me that you didn't do a bit of work, that you just played ball."

"Well, that wasn't my fault. I went there to work. If my boss didn't give me anything to do, that was his problem."

Chip shook his head hopelessly. "No, it's your problem. And besides, you know that's not really true."

Wilder gestured contemptuously. "It gets around all that stuff."

"Not in my opinion."

"Who's asking you?"

"No one," Chip said thoughtfully. "I'm not worrying about you, Wilder. But when it comes to the team and the school, well, that's different."

Chip tapped the piece of paper. "According to the manual, the NCAA can deprive a school of any victories and its conference standing if an ineligible player represents the college in games against other member college teams."

Chip paused and eyed Wilder hopefully. "There it is,

in black and white. Think what it would mean to the rest of the guys if something like that happened."

Wilder brushed the statement aside. "How could anything happen?"

"Easy. Someone could report you to the NCAA or to the school, and the whole season would be ruined, for everybody. That would be a terrible mistake."

"Look, Chip," Wilder said persuasively, "*you're* the one who's making the mistake. You're halfway through college, or you will be in a couple of months. Why don't you cash in now? What if you got hurt? You'd never have a chance to make any of that big money."

Chip shook his head decisively. "You just don't understand. I'm not interested in playing baseball for money until I get through school. I love baseball, but I've never thought about it as a career."

Wilder couldn't understand it. "But you can do both," he persisted.

"I don't want to do both," Chip said patiently. "I'm interested in only one thing—graduating from college with my degree in chemistry. If I can have some fun playing college baseball, fine. But if it comes to a choice between baseball and college, I'll quit baseball!"

CHAPTER 7

A Battle
between Pitchers

SOAPY WAS up early Sunday morning and back with the papers before Chip was awake. He slipped quietly into the room and opened up the *Herald* to the sports pages. What he found there overpowered his usual thoughtfulness, and he shook Chip awake. He pointed to a headline:

SOPHOMORES DOMINATE STATE
BASEBALL SCENE

"How about that? Now listen! Listen to this! 'Henry Rockwell's intrasquad series has clearly proved that the sophomores up from the great freshman team of a year ago must be given serious consideration for regular berths on the varsity team.' How do you like that?"

"I like it," Chip said, scrambling out of bed.

"Now here's the best part of all," Soapy continued. "'Chip Hilton rates on a par with the great senior hurler, Hector "Hex" Rickard, and the other two sophomore pitchers, Rod "Diz" Dean and Terrell "Flash" Sparks, are sure to see a lot of action.' Pretty good, huh?"

"Pretty good," Chip agreed, nodding.

"There's more," Soapy said, leaping on his bed and striking a comical pose. "Get this! 'Widow Wilder, veteran catcher, will have lots of support from a red-headed receiver who looks ready to handle any assignment.'" Soapy bowed to an imaginary audience before continuing. "'Soapy Smith, who was Hilton's receiver last year with the freshmen Fence Busters, is smart and agile, possesses a fine arm, and is strong with the stick.'"

Soapy grinned in delight and vaulted over the footboard of his bed. Then he walked in front of the mirror and posed again. "Me!" he yelped. "I'm smart! Wait until I show *that* to my abnormal psychology prof! Wait, she's not abnormal; the class is abnormal," Soapy quipped, quickly moving his eyebrows up and down. "No, that's not right either." Soapy laughed, still posing in front of the mirror. "We're *all* abnormal!" Chip groaned at Soapy's antics and winged a pillow in his direction.

At the same time, another pitcher-catcher combination was talking about the newspaper stories. However, those two weren't having as good a time over it.

Widow Wilder and Doogie Dugan were sitting in the airport terminal sipping coffee from Styrofoam cups and reading the *Herald* while waiting to meet someone due in on the next flight from Chicago. Dugan finished the article and tossed the paper aside. "Rockwell must have written that," he growled.

"Oh, I don't know," Wilder said lightly. "You wouldn't be a little hot because your name was left out, would you, Doogie?"

Dugan shrugged. "Of course not. Come on, tell me who you're expecting on this flight."

"I told you before. An important guy."

"Who?"

"Look, Doogie, it's personal. I told you that."

"But why so mysterious? You act as if it's a big secret."

"It is. That's why I didn't want you to come along."

Dugan's face flushed in sudden anger. "Why didn't you tell me?"

"I tried to, but—"

"You act as if you think I can't keep my mouth shut."

"I know, Doogie, but this is different."

"I bet it's somebody big in baseball. Right?"

"Right!"

"I'd like to meet him. Look, Widow, you can trust me."

Wilder deliberated. "Well, all right. I'll introduce you to him."

There weren't very many passengers arriving from Chicago, but one man attracted notice as he left the jetway and started to walk along the concourse. His expensive clothes and bold confidence marked him as a man accustomed to attention.

"That's him! That's Jon Hart," Wilder said exultantly. "He used to play in the majors, and he knows all kinds of important people in the game."

Wilder walked up rapidly and grasped Hart's hand. "Glad you made it, Jon," he said warmly. "This is Doogie Dugan. He's the junior college pitcher I was telling you about."

Dugan beamed and shook Hart's hand warmly. "I'm sure glad to meet you," he said.

Wilder picked up Hart's suit bag, and the three walked slowly to the airport hotel, which was just off the west concourse.

A BATTLE BETWEEN PITCHERS

Dugan was enthralled. He pressed close to Hart's side and hung on every word the man uttered.

"Well, Wilder," Hart said expansively, "what have you got to report?"

"He's the greatest, Jon. I watched him last year as a freshman, but this year I've seen him up close. There isn't any question about it. He's the best I ever saw."

"That's a pretty strong statement."

"Wait until you see him," Wilder said quickly. "He's got everything. I caught Rusty Gainor last summer, and Rusty couldn't carry this guy's glove!"

Dugan had been listening avidly, thrilled to be in the company of the man Wilder had spoken about so often. Now his curiosity got the best of him. "Who are you talking about?" he asked.

"Hilton," Wilder said shortly. "Chip Hilton."

"Hilton?" Dugan echoed. "You mean you think he's a great pitcher? Just because of those seven innings he pitched the other day?"

"Nope," Wilder said curtly.

"Well, what's he done? What's he got?"

"Plenty!" Wilder said roughly. "Look, Doogie, Mr. Hart and I have some business to talk over. I'll meet you at the car, or better yet, I might be awhile. You better grab a cab back to campus."

"But I thought—"

Wilder was irritated. "I said beat it, Doogie. Go on, get out of here."

Dugan glowered at Wilder and then stalked angrily away. But the glance he cast over his shoulder at Wilder was venomously vicious. "Some friend," he muttered angrily. Dugan was really hurt. Now for the first time Dugan had clear insight into Wilder's selfish character. "He's for Wilder, first, last, and all the time," the fiery little pitcher muttered. He walked to the long row of taxis lined up at the curb outside the terminal to catch one back to campus.

After Hart had checked in, he and Wilder went to the hotel restaurant and ordered coffee. Then they got down to the real purpose of Hart's trip to University.

"I got your fax," Hart said. "So here I am. What's the good word?"

"Like I wrote you, there are three or four good prospects here: a couple of good sophomore outfielders, Finley and Burke, and the big left-handed first baseman, Biggie Cohen, who's the best of the lot."

"Next to Hilton, you mean."

"That's right. Hilton and Cohen can't miss. I haven't had a chance to work on Cohen yet."

"How are you making out with Hilton?"

Wilder shook his head ruefully and told Hart about his talks with Chip. "He's the most stubborn guy I ever met," he concluded.

"What about Cohen?"

"I haven't talked to him. But he's real good friends with Hilton."

After a short pause, Hart said thoughtfully, "About Hilton, maybe you'd better go easy with him. You didn't mention any details like players' names, did you? Or tell him you got paid or signed a contract?"

Wilder shook his head uncertainly. "Well, not exactly. I told him I had a summer job and played with some other college guys."

"That was a little risky, Wilder. You'd better stop talking about summer ball for a while. By the way, I'm leaving town tomorrow night. I'll be back next Saturday to see your first game."

The big man picked up the check and nodded

again at Wilder. "Take care of yourself and keep out of trouble."

On Monday afternoon, long before the players arrived for the intrasquad game, Jon Hart made sure he had a good seat in the grandstand directly behind home plate. The fans filled the stands quickly. Cindy Collins and her dad, clutching bags of peanuts, waved to a few friends and then took their customary seats in the second row behind home plate. By the time the teams came out on the field, the grandstand and the bleachers along first and third bases were jammed. This game was for blood; it was the test of the real ballplayers, and the fans wanted to see them in action in the showdown game.

Chip warmed up with Soapy while Wilder directed the infield and outfield practice. Over in front of the other dugout, Al Engle was warming up Hex Rickard. Once, between warm-up throws, Hex caught Chip's eye and smiled. Then he good-naturedly shook a fist at Chip.

"He's a great guy," Chip muttered.

A few minutes later, Wilder and Hex met at the plate with the umpires to decide which squad would be considered the home team. Wilder won the toss and chose last bats. Seconds later, Chip was standing on the mound, fingering the ball and smoothing the dirt around the pitching rubber with the toe on his right shoe.

"All right, Chip!" Wilder called. "Let me have that ball!"

Chip took his warm-up throws and then stepped behind the rubber and glanced around the infield. Speed and Crowell and Andre Durley had finished their infield throws, too, and they all crowded around him.

"Let's go, man," Crowell said spiritedly.

"We'll get them," Durley said firmly. "You just fire those pitches in there."

PAY-OFF PITCH

"This is it, Chipper," Speed said, clasping Chip's hand in friendship and support. A lot was riding on the outcome of this game, and they all knew it.

Then, from the dugout, Soapy added his shout of encouragement: "We'll kill 'em, Chipper baby! Can't hit 'em if they can't see 'em!"

The plate umpire handed a new ball to Wilder, and the big receiver walked halfway up the alley as he polished the ball. "Nothing to it," he said. He tossed the ball to Chip and turned back to his position.

Russ Merton led off for Rickard's team. Chip studied the veteran shortstop as he crouched over the plate. Wilder called for a fastball, but Chip shook him off. "Merton will be looking for that," he breathed. "I've got to get off to a good start." He settled for a slow curve, and it caught the outside corner for a called strike.

Merton was determined to make Chip pitch. He crowded the plate with his elbows, bat, and head extending over the middle of the strike zone. Wilder fixed that; he called for a fastball, and Chip blazed one across the inside corner. Merton put on a good show, falling away in mock alarm. But the pitch was in there for another strike.

"Way ahead, Chip!" Wilder called gleefully.

"Atta baby, Chipper!" Soapy yelled.

The players in Rickard's dugout got on Chip, but he scarcely heard them. Wilder called for another fastball, and Chip blazed the ball at Merton's wrists. Merton again stepped back. At the last second he saw his mistake and tried for the hit. But he was too late, and Chip had his first strikeout.

Wilder gleefully sent the ball zipping around the bases and shook his fist at Chip. "Just what we need, man!" he yelled. "Easy pickings!"

A BATTLE BETWEEN PITCHERS

Minnie Minson had a good eye. The ball had to be right in there before he made a move. Wilder knew the veteran well and kept Chip's pitches low. With the count at two and two, Minson reached for an outside fastball. The result was a big hopper right to Chip. He took it on the first bounce and fired the ball to Harris for the second out. The fans let him know they liked the way he fielded the ball and made the throw to the keystone sack.

Belter Burke was up next, eager and determined. Chip got the big sophomore to reach for a high outside pitch for strike one. He followed with a slow, lazy curve for strike two. A change-of-pace ball, low and outside, made it one and two, and then he came back with a fireball that darted under Burke's wrists for the third strike. That made it three up and three down, and Chip had two strikeouts and an assist.

A joyful Soapy was out of the dugout with Chip's jacket before he got off the infield. "They couldn't even see it!" the redhead chortled.

Wilder had located Jon Hart in the grandstand before the game started. Now, as he walked toward the dugout, he looked in Hart's direction and nodded his head. Then he turned and slapped Chip on the back. "Nice going, Chip."

Ozzie Crowell was selecting a bat from the rack, and Wilder walked over beside him. "You're up, Ozzie. Work him. Let's see what he's got." Ozzie saw what Rickard had all right. So did everyone else! It was a lightning-fast ball that came out of nowhere and ended up untouched in Engle's glove. It took Rickard just four pitches to set Crowell down and send him back to the dugout.

Rickard got Speed the same way. Reggie Harris looked over a ball, took a called strike, and then met Hex's fastball a little late. The ball sped on a line for right field, but Biggie back-pedaled swiftly, leaped high in the air, and expertly speared the ball for the third out.

Chip kept up the pace in the second inning. He got ahead of Biggie on a knee-high called strike, and when his pal went for a high one around the shoulders, the result was a foul ball that Wilder picked off the top of Rickard's dugout.

Fireball Finley got too far under a change-of-pace ball, and Ozzie Crowell gathered in the blooper for the second out. Chip was really firing his pitches now, and he struck Bentley out on two called strikes and a slow curve that Bill missed by a ZIP code.

The fans applauded Chip when he went into the dugout. A few minutes later, they did the same for Hex Rickard. The likable senior duplicated Chip's effort, and it now became obvious to everyone that Chip and Hex were far ahead of the hitters. This game was going to be a battle between pitchers.

What It's Really
All About

JON HART was never modest about his knowledge of baseball. Now, surrounded by baseball fans, he was in his element. He leaned back expansively, rested his elbows on the back of his seat, and looked around. "Do you know the names of all the players?" he asked the fan beside him.

"You've definitely found the right man," someone behind him said. "He knows their ages, height, weight, how many hours they sleep at night, what they eat, and how many fillings they've got in their teeth."

That got Hart started, and he was soon talking to every fan who could hear him. There was no question about Hart's baseball knowledge, and it wasn't long before he had said just enough to plant the impression he was a major-league scout. Cindy Collins was surprised at her father's uncharacteristic silence.

"What do you think of the pitchers—Rickard and Hilton?" an awed fan asked.

Hart made sure the surrounding fans were listening before he answered. "Not bad," he said deliberately. "In fact, that's why I'm here."

"You mean you're here to look 'em over?"

Hart nodded. "Those two and a couple of others."

"Wilder's one of 'em, I'll bet," someone interposed.

"Could be that big sophomore first baseman too," another said.

"Yeah! Could be! How about *him?*"

Hart nodded. "He's not bad," he said carefully. "Not bad at all."

"What about the big center fielder on Rickard's team?"

"If you mean the guy who played fullback, I like him."

"How did you know he played fullback?"

"Oh, I get around," Hart said mysteriously.

Realizing Hart was talking about Fireball Finley, Cindy poked her father, "Dad!"

Jim Collins nodded quietly but made no comment.

As the game progressed, Hart added to the education of his listeners by calling the pitches and plays. And as the bitter duel between Chip and Rickard continued, he became more talkative. The fans ate it up.

Neither team scored in the first six innings. Chip had limited Rickard's team to one hit—a scratch single by Biggie Cohen—and tallied ten strikeouts. Hex Rickard had been touched for three solid blows, but brilliant support had smothered the scoring threats. Hex had six strikeouts to his credit.

In the top of the seventh, Rickard's heart of the order was up with Merton at bat, Minson on deck, and Belter Burke in the hole. Behind this formidable trio, Chip knew Biggie and Fireball were ready with their big bats, eager for a chance to win the game. "I'd better get the first three," he told himself.

WHAT IT'S REALLY ALL ABOUT

It was easier than Chip anticipated. He struck out Merton and Minson, and that left only Belter Burke.

Burke marched up for his third turn at bat, and Chip thought back to the two other times he had faced Belter. Each time, Burke had been too anxious.

"Maybe he'll go for a soft one," Chip breathed. He shook Wilder off until he got the sign for his lazy curve. He aimed it for Burke's elbows and let it go just as he would have released his fastball.

Burke was too anxious. He stepped into the pitch, but his swing was too fast and too hard, and he cut under the ball. He got a piece of it, but it was enough only to lift a high fly over Chip's head.

"Morris! Morris!" Wilder yelled. "Give him room!"

Chip moved out of the way, and Speed maneuvered until he was in position. The ball stayed up a long time, it seemed to Chip. But when it came down and smacked into his glove, Speed clutched it tightly and ran off the field. Three up and three down!

The sky was beginning to darken now, and Wilder hurried his hitters. "Come on! This is our last chance. We gotta do it now! We're only playing seven innings. You're up, Morris."

Speed walked out to the plate. Harris stood in the on-deck circle, swinging three bats. Gillen waited by the bat rack.

"Come on, Speed!" Soapy yelled. "Start it off!"

Rickard pitched for the corners, and Speed waited the pitches out. Then, with the count at three and two, Rickard called on his blinding speed to zip a fastball right past Speed for the third strike.

Wilder called time and walked out beside Harris. He talked to the player a moment and then turned toward the dugout. "Smith!" he bellowed. "Hit for Harris."

"Yes! Yee-ha!" Soapy screeched, scrambling along the dugout, tripping over his teammates' legs, and tugging up his pants. "You hear that, you guys? You just sit there and watch how ole Soapy does it."

"We'll wait," someone commented dryly.

"That's all I wanted to hear," Soapy said. "I'm on my way to first base right now."

"Sure," Dugan growled.

Soapy grinned and pointed his finger at the sarcastic hurler. "Wanna bet?"

Soapy Smith loved to kid around, but behind his generous good humor was a grim resolve to be a good baseball player. Soapy's carefree clowning usually overshadowed his deep desire. But he was serious now. This was his big chance.

Murphy Gillen was kneeling in the on-deck circle, and he shook his bat at Soapy. "You get on, you redheaded fool, and I'll bring you in."

"That a promise?"

Gillen nodded. "It's a promise."

Soapy got on. He crowded the plate for two straight pitches, and then one of Rickard's sharp slants caught him on the shoulder before he could duck out of the way. Soapy grimaced and rubbed his shoulder. He tossed his bat away and grinned at Gillen. "Well, big boy," he called over his shoulder as he headed for first base, "you called it! Nothing to do now but bring me home!"

Gillen wasn't much of a talker. He stood up, tossed the extra bats toward the dugout, and walked briskly up to the plate. Rickard knew all about the power packed in Gillen's bat, and he wasn't going to give the big outfielder anything good. And on the other side of the fence, Gillen wasn't going to go for anything bad! He worked Hex until the count was three and two. That left the decision up to Rickard.

WHAT IT'S REALLY ALL ABOUT

Hex decided to pitch to Gillen and tried to throw his fastball past him. That was a mistake. Gillen met the pitch with the meat of his bat, and the ball screeched out and up, up and out, and clear over the left-field fence.

Soapy touched all the bases and brought home the winning run. That run decided the series for Wilder's team, three games to two.

Chip, Speed, Wilder, Durley, and Crowell mobbed Soapy at the plate. The redhead shook hands gravely all around. Then he held up his hands for silence and waited for Gillen. "Hold it. I gotta make sure Murphy touched first base. He did, Mister Umpire? Thank you. Now, gentlemen, I give you Mister Delivery Boy himself. Meet Mister Kill 'Em Gillen!"

Gillen grabbed and shook Soapy's hand. "You did your part, Soapy," he said awkwardly. "I had to do mine."

The field cleared a lot more rapidly than the stands. The fans were still talking about Chip's and Rickard's great pitching. But Jon Hart was through with the gabbing. Jim Collins watched intently as the man took the stadium steps two at a time. Hart was eager to get back to the hotel to prepare for his talk with Chip Hilton.

After dinner, Hart packed his suit bag and spent an hour in his room. Then he set out for Grayson's. He made a few purchases from the pharmacy and paid for them at the cashier's desk. Mitzi Savrill was on duty and gave him his change.

"Is Chip Hilton around?" Hart asked.

"Why, yes, he is. He's in the stockroom. You go through that door there in the back of the store. Do you want me to call him?"

"No, thanks. I can find my way."

Hart walked to the back of the store and barged into the stockroom without knocking. Chip was all alone, sorting some invoices at his desk. "Hello, Hilton," Hart said, advancing across the room and extending his hand. "Remember me?"

Chip was caught by surprise, but he recognized Jon Hart immediately. "Yes, I do," Chip managed to respond carefully, remaining seated.

"Some game you pitched today."

"Did you see it?"

"I wouldn't have missed it. In fact, I came out here just to see it. Or I should say, to see you pitch."

"Me?"

"Now, Hilton, let's cut out this sparring. You know why I'm here—"

Chip had fully recovered his poise and shook his head. "If it's about summer baseball, Mr. Hart, I'm not—"

Hart raised a hand to silence Chip. "Now wait a minute. I've got a proposition you can't afford to pass up. You don't sign anything and you don't get any money. All you have to do is walk into your bank and let me put some money in an account in your mother's name. And—"

"I'm not interested, Mr. Hart."

"Now hold it! That money is in trust. It stays right there in your mother's name until the day you graduate. Then you and your mom can do anything you please with it."

"It's not right."

"Not right? There's nothing *wrong* with it! I'll be back here next Saturday, and I'll have your check." Hart turned and walked briskly to the door.

Chip got to his feet. "I won't—" It was too late; Chip was talking to himself. Hart kept right on going and closed the door firmly behind him.

Chip dropped back in the chair beside the desk. This was the second time someone had offered him money to sign a contract. Chip's thoughts flew back to Valley Falls to his first encounter. The man had come to his home one night and tried to get him involved in some scheme. That man had tried every way to get him to agree and had climaxed his efforts by upending a briefcase, spilling hundreds of twenty-dollar bills all over the floor.

"Man," he breathed, "I'm glad no one saw me talking to Hart."

Chip was upset by Hart's visit, and he was glad when Soapy and Fireball came rushing in with their usual abruptness. They were already changed out of their Grayson's uniforms.

"Come on, Chipper," Soapy said. "Let's get something to eat and go home. What a night!"

"You'd think it was the only place to eat in town," Fireball grumbled. Choosing Pete's Place for a sandwich was a mistake. At a booth near the door, a crowd of students surrounded Hex Rickard and Jim Locke, sports editor of the *News*.

Hector Rickard spotted them as soon as they entered. "Hey, Chip! Come on over. Hi ya, Soapy! Hi ya, Fireball! Come on, join us."

There was nothing they could do but join the crowd. After some good-natured ribbing from Hex and his friends, Jim Locke engaged in the conversation, directing his questions to Chip and Rickard. A minute or so after Chip and his pals joined the group, Doogie Dugan walked through the front door.

Unnoticed by the group, he sat down at the counter. Dugan was feeling sorry for himself. He hadn't gotten in the game, and he was still angry at Wilder because of the way he had brushed him off in front of Jon Hart. The sight of Chip, obviously the center of an admiring group, rekindled his resentment against the rival pitcher. But even as jealous anger flooded his thoughts, Dugan was forced to admit that Chip Hilton *was* a great baseball player. After he was served, he munched his sandwich and listened to the conversation.

"You looked awfully good this afternoon, Hilton. You, too, Rickard," Locke said.

"We were lucky," Chip said.

"The team looks a lot better this year, Hex," Locke ventured.

"It is better," Rickard said.

"Because of the sophomores?"

"That's right," Rickard said quickly. "Our pitching is going to be great. My friend Chip Hilton here is the best I ever saw in college."

"I don't see how anyone could improve on *your* record last year," Locke said.

Rickard laughed. "Me? I was terrible! I'm the one they knocked off the mound in the big game with A & M. Remember?"

"I remember," Locke replied. "But you had only two days' rest."

"Well, anyway," Rickard continued, "things will be different this year. We have a lot more power at the plate too. I think we'll win the conference title. In fact, I think we can win the national championship."

"I guess you've heard the rumors going around town that some of you college guys might be pros—"

Rickard bristled. "That's not true!" he said sharply. "I know *all* the guys. They're not that kind."

"Where there's smoke there's fire."

"Not where our guys are concerned," Rickard maintained stoutly. "Lots of us have had opportunities with the pros. Hilton's name would have been in the draft right out of high school, but he made it clear he wanted to come to college first. I've had some chances too. But there's one thing you have to understand about college ballplayers. They like to play baseball, all right, but there's more to it than that; they like to play college ball because it gives them a chance to do something for their school, for their community. It's a chance to show their appreciation and loyalty."

"You still feel that way, Hilton?"

"Yes, sir."

"You're not trying to tell me that school means more to you than baseball—"

"Yes, Mr. Locke. I am."

"Now, wait a minute—"

"I mean that, Mr. Locke," Chip said. "I love to play baseball, but right now my big ambition is to get a college degree."

"But baseball must have *some* place in your future plans."

"Sure. That's true enough, but right now I'm interested in school and, well, growing up."

"You really mean that, don't you?"

"I sure do."

"How about the rest of the sophomores?" Locke asked. "Do you think they feel the same way?"

"Yes, sir, I do."

"Then why do they play baseball?"

"It's actually pretty simple. They want to be on a team, to belong to something bigger than themselves. And they want to prove they can accept responsibilities and that they're men enough to keep trying when it looks as if they haven't got a chance. It's sort of a personal challenge, I guess."

"Do you think that applies to *all* the players? What about the ones who sit the bench?"

"I think it applies to any player who goes out for a team, whether he makes it or not. When a guy makes a State team, it means he's someone special. He's assumed a big responsibility whether he's a manager, a trainer, or a sub."

"Well," Locke said dryly, "he *should* feel that way, but I'm not convinced everyone does."

Unseen by the group, Dugan departed right after Chip finished talking. The little pitcher was doing some serious thinking. For the first time, Doogie Dugan began to understand what school loyalty, team play, sportsmanship, and college were all about.

CHAPTER 9

An Ineligible Player

COACH HANK ROCKWELL was up early Tuesday morning. The sky was clear, and the sun was shining brightly. After breakfast he drove across the campus to the field house. He parked his car and walked up to the coaches' office, whistling happily.

When Rock walked into the athletics office, Jim Corrigan was sitting beside an open window studying the baseball schedule. "Hi ya, Rock," he said, looking up. "You sound happy."

Rockwell yanked off his jacket and sat down at the desk. "Why not? It's a beautiful baseball day, and we've got a great ball club. What more could a coach want?"

"Competition," Corrigan said with a laugh. "By the way, did the series prove anything to you?"

"Plenty. Here's the varsity list, Jim. Ask Murph to post it before practice. That's one job I *always* hate."

"Got your lineup picked?"

"Just about," Rockwell replied thoughtfully.

"I'm listening," Corrigan said eagerly.

"Well, there's no question about the pitchers. Hex and Chip are tops. Dean and Sparks look all right too."

"What about Dugan?"

Rockwell deliberated. "Well," he said uncertainly, "Doogie seems to be a little mixed up."

"You mean he's feuding instead of chucking," Corrigan snorted.

"That's about it."

"What about the batting order?"

"I like Merton at shortstop and in the leadoff position; Minson at third base, hitting second; Bentley in left field, hitting third—"

"No question about the next two hitters," Corrigan interrupted. "Cohen and Finley. No competition there."

"Right."

"What about second base?"

Rockwell smiled and shook his head. "That's a tough one," he muttered. "Crowell looks mighty good, but I'm going with Ryder for the time being."

"That leaves right field and a receiver."

"I plan to go with Burke in right and Wilder, naturally, behind the plate."

"Smith looks good to me," Corrigan said tentatively.

"He is good, Jim. But Wilder has the experience. I've got to go with him," Rockwell ended decisively.

"How about Engle and Nickels?"

"Engle has a better arm and is a little stronger at the plate, but—"

"I know," Corrigan said understandingly. "He's mixed up too. Oh, I nearly forgot." He slid an envelope across the desk. "Found this under the door. It's addressed to you."

Rockwell opened the envelope and began reading the

contents. His face quickly darkened. "What in the world? Here, Jim, read this!"

Chip's Tuesday afternoon chemistry lab lasted until 3:30, and he was on his way as soon as the clock in the student union tower chimed the half-hour. Soapy and Speed had lab classes, too, but he didn't see them until he reached the field house. They were waiting on the steps.

"C'mon!" Soapy called excitedly. "Kelly said the varsity list was going to be posted this afternoon. *I'm* not worried though."

"Not much!" Speed added.

Soapy led the way and barged into the locker room. "Where is it, Murph?" he blurted out. "Where's the varsity list?"

Kelly shook his head in resignation and sighed. "You're on it, Smith. You, too, Chip, Speed."

"Yippee!" Soapy yelled. "We made it!"

Kelly silenced him gruffly. "Get over to the bleachers in the field house. All of you. The rest of the team just left. You can dress after the meeting."

As Chip and his two buddies entered the field house, they saw their teammates taking seats in the bleachers. Rockwell waited patiently until Chip, Soapy, and Speed were seated. "Men," he said, "I'm up against a tough problem. I don't know just how to handle it. Perhaps you can help."

The veteran coach paced back and forth several times. Then he stopped and pulled a note out of the pocket of his warm-up jacket. "I have a letter here stating that one of the players on this squad is a professional."

There was a short silence that was broken only by the shuffling of the feet of the players and the movement of their bodies as they shifted uneasily and covertly scanned the faces of their teammates.

"But," Rockwell continued abruptly, "I don't believe it! I don't think anyone here would palm himself off as an amateur if he had played pro ball, so I'm going to disregard this note. However, if any of you have played summer baseball under circumstances that might be even the least bit questionable, I want you to give me the details."

Rockwell paused to let that register before continuing. "We'll elect a captain Saturday. Right before the Cathedral game. All right, let's go."

Rockwell's announcement had quieted the players. But when they reached the field, their baseball enthusiasm soon returned. Chip was glad when practice ended because he couldn't get Wilder out of his thoughts. And it was the same that evening at work. Whenever there was a lull in the stockroom, he tried to study. But his thoughts always came back to the burly catcher. "It must be Wilder," he told himself. "If he plays in a single game—man, even in a single inning—he'll get the school into trouble."

When Chip and Soapy went back to their room in Jeff after work, Chip was tempted to tell Soapy all about Wilder, but his pal was bubbling with happiness because of his selection for the varsity. Chip decided to keep the problem to himself. "Maybe it will all be worked out by tomorrow," he muttered.

But Wednesday afternoon brought more bad news. Murph Kelly's face was grim as he advised the players to hit the bleachers as soon as they were dressed.

"Not again!" Engle cried. "What is this, baseball or a lecture course?"

"You'll find out!" Kelly growled, his eyes narrowing.

AN INELIGIBLE PLAYER

Chip knew Henry Rockwell about as well as any player can know his coach; he knew Rock's love for baseball and for the opportunities it gave him to develop sportsmanship and team play. One glance was all Chip needed to know that Henry Rockwell was deeply disturbed. It must have been evident to the other players, too, because they quieted instantly.

"Men," Rockwell said slowly, "when I got home last night, I found another note." He paused and scanned their faces, shifting his glance from player to player. "This has ceased to be a joke." The players listened soberly as he continued. "My hands are tied. I don't know whether any of you have played pro baseball or signed a contract or accepted money to play ball. I only know that I have received a note written by someone right here in these bleachers. It says that the writer will send me the names of several players, and it says that one of the players listed is a professional."

Rockwell paused and shook his head ruefully. "All I can do is appeal to the person who wrote this note to give me the complete details. Otherwise, I can do nothing. All right, let's get in some practice."

It was a fast practice. Rockwell was clearly disturbed by the notes and dismissed the squad early. Chip, Soapy, and Speed went back to the locker room. As he dressed, Chip thought about Rockwell's problem. Chip was convinced now that the writer was referring to Widow Wilder. But who was the writer? Who would know about Wilder? Chip considered Wilder's pals. Al Engle? No, not him. Engle was clearly in Wilder's corner. Doogie Dugan? No, not him either. What went for Engle went for Dugan. Who?

Chip reached a decision. He was going to have a showdown with Widow Wilder. Chip got his chance that evening. Once again, Wilder was in Pete's Place when Chip dropped in for a quick sandwich. This time, Chip was eager to join Wilder in a booth.

Wilder grinned. "Well, have you figured out who wrote the notes?"

"No, I haven't. But I think it's a dirty trick."

"Writing the notes or playing pro ball?"

"Both!"

Wilder grinned and pulled a small clipping out of his pocket. "Listen," he said cryptically, "and tell me if you think a hundred thousand dollars is a dirty trick." He tapped the clipping. "It says here that a high school kid out in St. Louis got a hundred-thousand-dollar bonus to sign a big-league contract. What's wrong with that?"

"Nothing."

Wilder shrugged. "So? What's the difference between you and him?"

"Plenty! He isn't in college, and he isn't going to try to play amateur ball."

"So what? A college degree isn't any more important than a high school diploma in the big leagues. Look at Mickey Mantle and guys like Babe Ruth. They never had college diplomas and look what they did."

"That was a long time ago, Wilder. And maybe they didn't want to go to college. I do."

"You're a chump. You could have both. Look at me—"

"That's what I wanted to talk to you about," Chip said quickly. "Those notes must refer to you."

"Why me?"

"Because you got paid and you played under a false name."

"Wait a minute. I didn't have anything to do with the way some jerk spelled my name. And as far as getting paid is concerned, everybody gets paid when they have a job."

AN INELIGIBLE PLAYER

"That isn't the way you told it to me."

"I was just kidding you."

"It isn't anything to kid about, Wilder. Frankly, I think you ought to tell the coach the same thing you told me and then resign from the squad."

Wilder laughed boisterously. "Are you crazy?"

"No, but you are if you think you can get away with it."

"Get away with what? Tell me, Hilton. Where did I play? Who paid me? How do you know I played under an assumed name? I could have been telling you all that stuff as just a big joke." Abruptly, Wilder's manner changed.

"Look," he said roughly, "I'm going to play out the season, and no one is going to stop me. We're a cinch to win the conference and maybe even the NCAA championship. Do you know what that means? No? Well, I'll tell you. It means that we're going to have every big-league scout in the country watching us. And I'm going to ride that State championship right into the majors on some big money. When you play on a championship team, you always get a better break. Me resign from the team? No way. I'm sticking with State."

"Even if you jeopardize the school's reputation?"

"How can I? No one has anything on me."

"Maybe not, but it's hard to believe—"

"What? What's hard to believe?"

"That a solid ballplayer like you can be so selfish."

Wilder grinned. "A guy has to look out for himself, Hilton. My old man's been preachin' that to me for years. Look! The college isn't going to take care of you after you get that diploma you're always talking about."

Chip was suddenly filled with a strong dislike for Mitch "Widow" Wilder. "I don't know whether you're a professional or not, Wilder," he said angrily, "but if I knew for sure you *were* a pro, I'd tell everybody in town."

Chip turned and walked swiftly away. Wilder stared after him in open-mouthed surprise. "I believe he would," the big catcher muttered. "I believe he really means it."

CHAPTER 10

An Anonymous Letter

STATE FACULTY ROW was a pleasant little street, and Henry Rockwell and Mrs. Rockwell were happy in their home. But this evening was different. When the worried coach reached the house, he found the promised letter waiting for him on the table in the living room. And, as the anonymous writer had pledged, it listed five of his players—five of his best players.

The note spoiled Rockwell's dinner, and he spent the entire evening thinking over the problem. He read the note over and over and tried to work out a solution. Now, with Mrs. Rockwell looking over his shoulder, the coach read the note again.

> *Dear Coach Rockwell,*
> *One of the following players is a professional. He played for money last year under an assumed name:*

PAY-OFF PITCH

Biggie Cohen
Fireball Finley
Chip Hilton
Widow Wilder
Hex Rickard

Rockwell crumpled the note in his hands. Then he thought better of it and smoothed out the paper. Mrs. Rockwell patted him on the shoulder. "What are you going to do, Henry?"

"I don't know."

"Have you talked to Dad Young?"

"The other day."

"What did he say?"

"Said for me to use my own judgment. But, of course, to let him know as soon as I had anything concrete."

While this conversation was going on in Henry Rockwell's home, Chip was enduring a long, tiring evening, berating himself for waiting so long to tell Henry Rockwell about Jon Hart.

"I'll fix that," Chip promised himself. "I'll tell him tonight."

For the first time since he began working at Grayson's, Chip beat the clock. He met Soapy, Whitty, and Fireball at the fountain just as they were starting for the stockroom. "I've got to go on an errand, guys. See you later."

"I'll go with you," Soapy volunteered.

"No, Soapy. Thanks, but I have to go alone. Go on back to the dorm, and I'll be there soon."

A few minutes later Chip arrived at the brick house the Rockwells called home. He was relieved to see the lights gleaming. Moments after Chip rang the doorbell, Rockwell opened the door. "Hey, Chip! Come in. Chip is here," he called over his shoulder to Mrs. Rockwell.

AN ANONYMOUS LETTER

Mrs. Rockwell greeted Chip warmly and, despite his protests, departed for the kitchen "to round up something to snack on." Chip seized this opportunity to tell his old coach about Jon Hart. However, he avoided all reference to Widow Wilder.

When Chip finished, Rockwell nodded approvingly. "You did the right thing, Chip. He's trouble. Big trouble."

"He sure caught me by surprise. Do you think he'll really be back Saturday with a check?"

Rockwell nodded. "Yes, I think he will."

Chip smiled grimly. "He's sure persistent."

Rockwell leaned back in his chair and pulled the note out of his pocket. "Looks as if we both have our troubles. Take a look at this."

Chip read the note incredulously, scanning over the names. "I can't believe it. It doesn't seem possible."

"It's possible, all right. But this is *my* headache. Don't say anything about it to anyone."

"You can be sure of that."

Mrs. Rockwell returned then with sandwiches, cake, and milk, and Rock changed the subject. Chip left shortly afterward. He walked swiftly down the driveway and broke into a trot. Directly behind him, yet shielded by the darkness, a group of students were approaching, laughing and talking. Chip scarcely glanced at them as he took off for Jeff.

Soapy was reading at his desk when Chip entered the room. He closed the book with a snap and studied Chip intently. "What's going on?" he demanded. "What are you worrying about?"

"Nothing much."

"Who are you kidding? Come on. Maybe I can help."

"You can't help me right now, Soapy. It's something I've got to work out myself."

"Two heads are better than one."

But Chip wasn't persuaded, and Soapy had to be content with Chip's promise to share the problem when the need arose.

After Chip left, Mrs. Rockwell continued the discussion of the notes with her husband. "Aren't you placing a little too much importance on an anonymous letter, Hank?" she asked.

"No, I don't think so. This thing could jeopardize the school's eligibility."

"Well," Mrs. Rockwell said seriously, "I'm sure you'll work it out all right, Hank. You have a way of doing that. Maybe a good night's sleep will help you solve it."

Henry Rockwell didn't find sleep much help. In fact, he couldn't get to sleep. And when practice time rolled around the next afternoon, he was still wrestling with the problem of the anonymous note instead of concentrating on plans for the initial game of the season.

Jim Corrigan recognized the signs. "Now what?" he asked.

"Another letter," Rockwell said. "Here! Read it."

Corrigan read the letter and snorted in disgust. "Ignore it, Rock. Forget it."

"I can't just ignore it, Jim. It might be true."

"You're not a mind reader, Rock."

"I wish I were. Well, let's go. Kelly told the players to meet at the bleachers again."

The players were already seated in the field-house bleachers when Rockwell and Corrigan arrived. The Rock got right to the point. "I realize you're fed up with these notes as much as I am. However, something has to be done."

Rockwell read the note and then announced, "I want the five players named in the note to report to my office right away. The rest of you may as well know it now as later. None of the five players will play in a game until the matter is cleared up. I'll expect each of you to keep this matter confidential. All right, Jim, take over."

Chip was the last to see Henry Rockwell. When he entered the office, Rockwell smiled shortly. "I had to ask all five of you, Chip. Anyway, I've gotten exactly no place. Maybe it's all a hoax. I wish I knew. You go ahead out to practice."

Wilder was waiting when Chip came out of the office and fell in step beside him. "Well," he said lightly, "did you confess?"

"I didn't have anything to confess," Chip said coolly. "How about you?"

Wilder grinned. "Me? What *could* I confess?"

"I wish I knew," Chip said shortly, brushing past Wilder.

Widow Wilder met Jon Hart at the airport Friday night and accompanied him to his hotel. Over a sandwich in the hotel grill, Wilder talked about his conversations with Chip. Then he told Hart about the notes and Rockwell's decision not to use the five players.

"You think he means it?" Hart asked.

"I don't know. I don't know him that well yet, but Rockwell doesn't seem like the type of coach to say something he doesn't mean."

"Who do you think wrote the notes?" Hart asked abruptly.

"I haven't any idea."

"How about Hilton?"

"Well, he, Al Engle, and Doogie Dugan are the only ones I ever told about playing pro ball—"

"How about Engle and Dugan?"

Wilder shook his head and smiled confidently. "Wouldn't be either one of them, but I don't know about

Hilton. He's been riding me pretty hard. Wants me to quit the team. We kind of got into it last night. And when I was going home, I saw him coming out of Rockwell's house."

"That's bad," Hart said thoughtfully. "I was planning to see him tomorrow night. Now I don't know."

"He's the greatest," Wilder said wryly. "I sure wish you could convince him to play ball with us."

"Well, I haven't got much to lose," Hart said lightly. "I'll give it a try."

"I'd better start back to the dorm," Wilder said. "Big day tomorrow, the first game of the season. Oh, yeah, the team's electing a captain tomorrow before the game, and—"

"And you're it."

"Right," Wilder grinned. "At least, that's what the guys say. Well, see you tomorrow night."

Saturday was a perfect day for baseball. The sun was shining brightly and the temperature was in the high sixties. The fans came out in droves to see State's first game of the season.

The locker room was filled with the babble of voices when Rockwell and Corrigan entered. Murph Kelly got the attention of the players, and Corrigan distributed paper and pencils while Rockwell talked.

"As you know," the veteran coach said softly, "one of the great traditions here at State is the election of a captain in the locker room just before the first game. All of you are considered members of the varsity and are eligible to vote." He turned to the trainer. "Pull that board over here, will you, Murph? Thanks. Now I'd like to have the nominations."

Diston and Engle got to their feet at the same time. "Hex Rickard," Diston said.

AN ANONYMOUS LETTER

"Widow Wilder," Engle said loudly.

Rockwell wrote the two names on the board and waited expectantly. Then Soapy stood up. "Chip Hilton," he said clearly.

The coach wrote Chip's name on the board and turned back to face the players. "Any others?" he asked.

There were no other nominations, and Rockwell moved away from the board. "Choosing a good captain is important to all of us," he said slowly. "Choose a good one. Write in the name of your choice on the paper and fold it up."

Corrigan waited a few seconds and then collected the votes in his baseball cap. He handed the cap to Murph Kelly and opened the paper slips one at a time. Rockwell waited, prepared to mark the votes on the board.

"Wilder," Corrigan called. "Rickard . . . Wilder . . . Hilton." He continued to call out the votes.

Rickard was out of the running from the first as the votes for Chip and Wilder piled up. They ran neck and neck right up to the last vote. With the count at ten votes each, Corrigan opened the final slip of paper and handed it to Rockwell for verification. Then Coach Rockwell walked over in front of Wilder and held out his hand. "Congratulations, Wilder," he said, pulling the big player to his feet. "Men, your new captain."

Wilder's friends crowded around him, patting his shoulder and shaking his hand. When they quieted, Rockwell continued. "This is our first game, men, and I hope we get off on the right foot. Unfortunately, there's nothing new to report with respect to the notes. This means the five listed players will not be participating. All right, let's go."

So Chip, Biggie, Rickard, Finley, and Wilder sat deep in the dugout while their teammates warmed up for the game. The ball zipped around the horn following Rockwell's fungoes to the infield—to Minson on third, to Merton at short, to Ryder in the keystone slot, over to Reggie Harris on first, and back to the plate and Darrin Nickels.

Over on the other side of the plate, Corrigan was lifting high flies to Bentley, Reed, and Diston in the outfield. In front of the dugout, Diz Dean, Doogie Dugan, and Terrell Sparks were alternating their throws to Soapy.

Biggie nudged Chip. "He's starting all the upperclassmen," he said significantly.

"I don't get it," Wilder grouched angrily. "I get elected captain of the team, but because some jerk sent the coach an unsigned note, the guts of the ball club sits in the dugout!"

CHAPTER 11

Suspicions Grow

STATE'S BASEBALL FANS gave the Statesmen a rousing send-off as they charged out of the dugout to take the field. When the cheers died away, however, some of the more zealous fans began to check the lineup.

"Hey, where's Wilder? How come Nickels is catching?"

"Beats me. I thought Rickard or Hilton would be pitching."

"Look who's on first base! Man, Harris is Little League compared to Biggie Cohen."

"You've got that right!"

"Where's Fireball Finley?"

"They were out there warming up before the game."

"I see them! They're in the dugout."

Diz Dean burned the first pitch across the plate then, and the students in the stands forgot the questions and got behind their team. Dean was wild, and Cathedral took full advantage of his erratic pitching. Two walks and an advance bunt, which Diz fumbled, filled the bases. Then the Cathedral cleanup hitter got hold of one of Dean's fastballs and drilled a three-bagger against the right-field fence. Three runners scored.

Before the side was retired, two more runs were scored. It was a bad start! State was held scoreless in its turn at bat, and the first inning ended with Cathedral ahead, 5-0. That first inning set the pattern for five straight innings. Rockwell sent in a new battery then, with Soapy behind the plate and Doogie Dugan on the mound. Cathedral was leading, 8-3.

Dugan's twisters held Cathedral until the top of the ninth. Then the visitors got to him for three straight hits, filling the bases. The next hitter worked Dugan until the count was evened up at two and two. Then Dugan put all he had into a twister that was low outside and in the dirt.

The batter was smart; he saw that Soapy couldn't make the catch, punched at the ball, and headed for first base. Behind him, Soapy chased the ball to the screen. The third-base runner scored, leaving the bases still filled.

Dugan covered the plate and took Soapy's peg. He waited there until the redhead came trotting up. Then Doogie shocked Soapy out of his precious blue baseball socks. "It was my fault, Soapy. I threw it away."

Soapy could only stare at the little pitcher. It was the first time Dugan had ever spoken to him without bitterness. They stood there for a short second before Soapy recovered his voice. "Time!" he called to the umpire. Then he followed Dugan partway up the alley. "I called the pitch, Doogie," he said. "It was my mistake, but it won't happen again."

"Thanks, Soapy," Dugan said quietly. "I'll get them now. That run is *all* they're going to get."

Dugan was right. He struck out two consecutive hitters and then forced the next batter to hit a high fly between the plate and the pitcher's box. Soapy motioned everyone away and gathered in the ball for the third out. Then he and Dugan walked off the field side by side like old friends.

Down in the dugout, Al Engle and Widow Wilder watched Dugan and Soapy in unmasked surprise. "Look at that," Engle breathed, shaking his head. "All buddy buddy."

Wilder nodded slowly and said, "Something new has been added."

Rockwell was up and out of the dugout. "All right, men," he said. "Last licks! Now or never."

"Right!" Corrigan chorused. "We can still do it."

But it wasn't to be. The Cathedral pitcher mowed the State hitters down one-two-three, and the game ended with a final score of Cathedral 11, State 3.

Chip, Biggie, and Fireball caught up with Soapy and Dugan and walked along with them to the locker room. Chip was as surprised as Engle and Wilder at Dugan's turnaround. His new attitude was completely out of character, and conversation was difficult. Henry Rockwell and Jim Corrigan followed closely behind them, accompanied by two curious sportswriters.

"How come you didn't use Rickard, Coach?" one asked.

"Or Hilton?" the other added.

"I can't answer that now," Rockwell said quietly.

"How about Wilder?"

"And Cohen and Finley. You sure could have used their hitting."

"I know," Rockwell said shortly, "but it's a long season. There's plenty of time."

The players were quiet and subdued until they reached the locker room. Some of them banged their shoes against their lockers then, grumbling in disgust. Wilder and Al Engle took the lead, directing their verbal ire toward Henry Rockwell.

Chip and his pals didn't like it, but they said nothing. They dressed as quickly as possible and left together. Once they were outside on the street, however, their tongues loosened. Biggie Cohen was boiling with anger, restraining himself only with difficulty. "*That* was hard to take," he growled.

"It sure was," Chip agreed. "But an argument wouldn't help."

"You think Rock is doing the right thing?" Schwartz asked.

"He *always* does the right thing," Soapy said quickly.

A few blocks later, Biggie, Speed, and Red Schwartz cut across the campus toward Jeff while Chip, Soapy, and Fireball continued on their way to work.

Chip's first lull in his work at Grayson's came around eight o'clock. His assistant, Isaiah Redding, went around the corner to Pete's Place for a burger. Chip sat down and began thinking about the anonymous notes. From the notes, it was a quick leap to think of Jon Hart. Chip realized suddenly that the talkative man had promised to be back this very day with a check.

Then, as if on cue, the door opened. Hart swaggered into the room. "Well, Hilton, here I am!"

Before Chip could rise to his feet, Hart had reached the desk, grasped his hand, and shook it vigorously.

"Bet you thought I was kidding," he said. He fished an envelope out of his pocket and slapped it on the desk. "Open it, Hilton!"

Chip started to rise. "I—"

"Never mind," Hart said. "I'll open it myself."

He opened the envelope and thrust a check into Chip's hand. "There!" he said dramatically.

Chip pushed the check back. "Wait—"

SUSPICIONS GROW

"Sure, you wait," Hart said quickly. "You wait two years. Until you graduate! But it's all yours. In *your* bank, in your mother's name."

Hart's flamboyant entry and sudden attack had thrown Chip completely off balance. Up to now, he hadn't been able to get in a word. "No!" Chip said firmly, standing up and dropping the check on the desk. "I wouldn't touch it."

"But I thought—"

"You thought wrong! I'm not interested!"

"Not interested in all that money?"

"*No, sir!*" Chip said decisively as he moved toward the door. "Right now I'm not interested in anything except graduating from State."

"But—"

"No buts, Mr. Hart," Chip said, stopping at the door. "You're wasting your time. Sorry." Chip hurried through the door and out the side entrance to Tenth Street, determined to escape the persistent man.

Later that night, Hart met Widow Wilder at the hotel and told him about Chip and the check. "I couldn't get him," he said ruefully. "He's the toughest."

"I told you that. Now what?"

"Plenty. I've got to finish up my plans for a trip to South America. Then I've got to look over those two kids down at Southwestern."

"I wish I could go to South America," Wilder said enviously.

"You stay here and keep me posted on Cohen, Finley, Burke, and Crowell. I'll be back two or three times to check them in action."

"When are you leaving?"

"Monday night."

"Are you giving up on Hilton?"

Hart shrugged his shoulders and smiled. "For the time being. Why?"

"Well, I was thinking if you made a point of being seen with him a couple times, it might draw a little of the heat away from me."

Hart grinned appreciatively. "Yeah. Sure! I get it. Everybody will think he's the player the note refers to."

Wilder nodded. "Exactly."

Jon Hart did a lot of talking around University on Sunday and Monday. He mingled with fans, students, and baseball sportswriters who remembered him from his playing days. He was extremely clever at leading his listeners into a baseball discussion and then helping them "discover" that he was someone important in professional baseball. He was just vague enough that they never did know exactly what he *did*. But whatever it was, his listeners knew it was pretty impressive. They were convinced he had important connections to some of the best professional teams in the country.

Yes, he was here to look over a couple of the State players. No, he wouldn't say exactly who.

When the varsity reported for practice Monday afternoon, Hart was in the stands, surrounded by a group of admiring students and fans. Yes, he knew all about the State players. That was the reason he was in town. He gestured toward Chip and Hex, who were throwing to Wilder in front of the bleachers. "Not bad, eh?"

"Which one?" a fan asked curiously.

Hart grinned. "Now that I can't exactly say." Just before the end of practice, Hart left his audience and sauntered down to the small iron gate leading from the grandstand to the field. The fans watched him avidly and speculated on the big-league prospect this great man was scouting.

SUSPICIONS GROW

Chip was on his way to work as soon as Rockwell's whistle ended the drill. He tucked his glove under his arm and headed for the hill leading to the field house. He was tired and in a hurry, and Hart's appearance surprised him. Hart stepped through the gate and fell into step beside Chip.

"Hello, Hilton," Hart said easily. "Mind if I walk along with you?"

Chip did mind. He made a move to walk around the obnoxious man, but Hart changed direction quickly and moved close beside him.

"Look, Hilton," Hart cajoled. "I just wanted you to know that I think you're doing the right thing by staying in school. You're absolutely right about it."

"I'm glad you think so."

"Well, I do. And I want you to know that I admire your independence. Not many kids would turn down money. More power to you."

"Thanks, Mr. Hart. Now I've got to—"

"I know, you've got to hurry back to work. Well, so long, kid. You're a great pitcher." Hart held out his hand, and Chip shook it quickly. Then the man grinned and turned back to the grandstand.

Hart left town that night, disappointed by his inability to convince Chip to come on board. But he was highly gratified by the impact he had made on University's students and fans as a pro-baseball representative. He was pleased, too, with his part in Wilder's little scheme to involve Chip Hilton. He had planted just enough curiosity and half-truths in the minds of those he had met to sow the seeds of suspicion. In practically every instance, Hart had left his listeners with the impression that Chip Hilton was now or was about to become big-league property.

PAY-OFF PITCH

The fans in the stands had seen the brief encounter and the seemingly friendly handshake between this colorful man and Chip Hilton. Most of the players had noticed it too. Soapy caught up with Chip right after Hart walked away, a deep scowl on his face. "What did that guy want?" he asked.

"Nothing, Soapy. He was just saying good-bye. He's leaving town tonight."

"It's not soon enough," Soapy growled.

Widow Wilder was quick to draw the attention of the players near him to the incident. "Well, what d'ya know," he said significantly. "Chip Hilton and a pro scout."

Chip was too worried about Widow Wilder to think much about the Hart incident. But by Tuesday afternoon, with the exception of his buddies, he was conscious of a change in his teammates' attitudes toward him. Widow Wilder said nothing, but he avoided Chip whenever he could. This was such an about-face that it attracted more attention than an open break.

Wilder's aloofness meant nothing to Chip. In fact, he was glad the burly catcher was keeping out of his way. But it was obvious to everyone that Soapy was upset by the turn of events. The usual comic was tight-lipped and grim all through the workout. Every time Soapy pegged the ball to a teammate, he fired it with all his power. His behavior was so completely out of character that his teammates were shocked.

That night, when Chip and Soapy reached Jeff, Soapy could stand it no longer. "Enough is enough, Chip! It's all right for a guy to prove he can take it, but there comes a time when he ought to give it too."

"What do you mean, Soapy?"

"Wilder!" Soapy exploded. "He's behind this professional deal and you know it."

"That could be."

"Could be? Could be? He is! He's the professional the note refers to—"

"But you don't *know* it, Soapy. You're just guessing."

"Maybe I am," Soapy countered, "but *you're* not."

"What can I do, Soapy? I haven't a shred of proof. All we can do is wait. There's bound to be a showdown in a day or two."

Wednesday afternoon, just before the game with Wesleyan, Rockwell told the squad that the five players would again watch the game from the dugout, because no one had come forward to admit his guilt.

The stands were not as full as they had been for Saturday's game, but it was a good weekday turnout. But when Chip, Ilex, Wilder, Biggie, and Fireball did not play, the fans began to wonder what it was all about. And when Wesleyan jumped out in front and led all the way, with none of the five stars appearing in the game, the fans became explosive and bitter. Henry Rockwell was their chief target. The final score: Wesleyan 12, State 5.

At the end of the game, the reporters were again waiting for the veteran coach. This time they were direct and insistent.

"Come on, Coach. Give! What's wrong?"

"Why so secretive? What did they do? Break training?"

"They must be ineligible, then—"

"There's a rumor going around town that you're keeping them out of the games because they're pros. Is that true?"

"What about Hilton? He's been seen in the company of a man who's supposed to be some kind of scout. Is he big-league property or not? Come on. What's the score?"

CHAPTER 12

A Life Turned Around

UNIVERSITY'S NEWSPAPERS, the *News* and the *Herald,* had fine sports sections and were up to the minute on local and national news. Jim Locke, the sports editor of the *News,* was extremely interested in State sports. He had been critical of Chip's knee injury during basketball season, mistakenly believing that Chip had been more interested in his national marksmanship title than the basketball team. When Dr. Mike Terring, State's medical director, showed Locke he was wrong, the caustic writer became one of Chip's strongest boosters. So when the sports editor knocked on the door to the stockroom that evening and paused in the doorway, Chip was pleasantly surprised.

"Hello, Chip," Locke said. "The cashier told me I could come right in." Chip shook his hand and gestured toward a chair. "Hi, Mr. Locke. Please sit down."

Locke sat down and looked around the room. "So this is where you hang out." He glanced at the open chemistry books on the desk. "Gives you a chance to do a little studying, too, I see."

Chip nodded. He knew this was not a social visit. And he knew that Jim Locke had earned his reputation of being able to smell out a sports story. *It's the anonymous notes,* Chip realized.

Locke evidently sensed Chip's thoughts. He nodded. "Yes," he said, "you're thinking right. I'm sorry to have to say this, Chip, but there's a rumor going around that Rockwell isn't using you, Rickard, Wilder, Cohen, or Finley because one of you is supposedly under contract or was made to play ball somewhere."

Chip nodded. "I know, Mr. Locke."

"The worst part of it," Locke continued, eyeing Chip intently, "is that everyone thinks *you* are the player involved and that Rockwell is trying to protect you because you played for him in high school."

"That isn't true. Coach wouldn't protect me or anyone else in something like this. There's too much at stake."

"I agree. I'm just telling you the rumors. Now one more thing. Have you ever played summer ball for pay or signed any kind of contract?"

Chip's intent look matched Locke's, steadily boring into his eyes. "No, Mr. Locke, I have not," Chip enunciated slowly and distinctly.

Locke nodded his head. "I'm glad to hear you say that. By the way, I want you to know that I think Coach Rockwell is doing the right thing. He's got to protect the program and the school."

"Thanks, Mr. Locke."

"Keep your chin up. This thing will come to a head pretty soon. Maybe tomorrow."

After Locke left, Chip tried hard to think of a solution to Rock's problem as well as his own. Suddenly, he snapped his fingers. "I've got it!" he breathed exultantly. "The AAU form, the amateur pledge! A signed pledge would clear everything up. I'll tell Rock tonight."

At closing time—right on the dot—Chip hurried out of the store. Soapy, Fireball, and Whitty were surprised. "Must be a fire!" Fireball said.

"Yeah," Whittemore agreed. "Wonder what's up! Come on, Soapy. What's the secret?"

"There's no secret, guys," Soapy said glumly. "He's just worried about you guys not being allowed to play ball."

Rockwell was at home and ushered Chip into the living room. "Mrs. Rockwell has gone to bed, Chip," he said, smiling, "but I think I can scare up some cake and hot chocolate."

"I'm not a bit hungry, Coach, and I've got a lot of studying to do. I thought of something that might help with the notes."

"That's good news. I'm stumped."

It didn't take Chip long to get his idea across to Rockwell, and when he left for Jeff, a great weight had been lifted from his heart. Rockwell's words stuck with him the rest of the evening: "You've hit it, Chip. There's not enough time to get the plan ready before we leave for Springfield tomorrow, but you can bet I'll have it set by Saturday. Don't say a word about this to anyone."

The Thursday papers carried the story of the Statesmen's second-consecutive defeat. In the face of the fabulous preseason predictions, these losses were shocking. The real dynamite was in the paragraphs dealing with the benching of five of State's brightest stars and Coach Henry Rockwell's "no comment" attitude. The sportswriters speculated about reasons, hinting vaguely at training infractions, insubordination, and scholastic difficulties.

A LIFE TURNED AROUND

When the players reported for practice that afternoon, they were worried and confused. Rockwell said nothing about the notes, and for all it accomplished, the practice might as well have been canceled. Now the cliques were working overtime. Wilder and his group stuck together like the four corners of the strike zone. As a result, Chip and Hex and their respective friends did the same.

At the end of the workout, Rockwell called a short meeting in the locker room to discuss the details of State's trip to Springfield for the game with Wilson University. "We leave tomorrow morning at 11:00. The following players will make the trip . . ." Rockwell read the names of the players, and when he finished, there was a stunned silence. None of the five benched players had been named. It was clear the Rock meant business.

"Our game on Saturday with Poly Tech is scheduled for 2:30. I want every player in this room to be in the lecture hall upstairs at twelve o'clock sharp. That's all."

Chip went straight to work after his last class on Friday afternoon and took over Soapy's duties behind the fountain. Fireball appeared a little later. The two friends put in a long afternoon wondering how the team was making out. The fountain was jammed at seven o'clock, but they still caught Gee-Gee Gray's sports broadcast. The news was bad. Wilson University had defeated State, 2-0. Sparks had pitched a six-hitter, and State had managed only two hits.

After work, Chip and Fireball walked over to Pete's Place. Despite the loss of the game, Fireball seemed upbeat and told Chip there was something important he needed to talk to him about. After the two friends ordered a pizza, Fireball cleared his throat and began.

"Chip, this isn't easy, but there's something I've been wanting to tell you. You know what a jerk I was last year during football season. No, wait," said Fireball, raising a hand in protest as Chip began to cut him off.

"Chip, I *need* to tell you this, so please listen. You might not even know it, but I was doing a lot of drinking then and got into some other stuff I'm not very proud of. And then I started using credit cards to buy things I didn't need with money I didn't even have. I was in way over my head.

"Anyway, the job you got me at Grayson's really helped a lot. But more than that, I watched you and Soapy and the rest of the guys, you know? How you live your lives. That turned me around, Chip."

Fireball met Chip's eyes. "So, here I am finally out of debt. And I'm happy, and I feel like for the first time in my life, I really know who I am and where I'm going. My grades are good, and I have a real vision for my future. And to a large extent it's because of you, Chip. Thank you. And . . . there's something else. If she'll have me, I plan to ask Cindy to marry me."

Chip could only smile at Fireball's words concerning his actions in the past year. But the news about Fireball and Cindy was wonderful! He reached across the table and grasped his friend's hand. "Congratulations, and I wish you all the best," said Chip. "It couldn't happen to a nicer guy."

On that note the two friends returned to Grayson's to finish the night, with each one reflecting on how fortunate he was to have the other as a pal.

On the way to Grayson's the next morning, Soapy told Chip about the game. "Rock started Sparks and Engle," he said, "and put me in for Al in the sixth. Sparks went the route, and was he right! He was bending 'em like a horseshoe, Chip, and the Wilson hitters couldn't do a thing with him. We just couldn't get Rock any runs."

A LIFE TURNED AROUND

Chip, Soapy, and Fireball left Grayson's at 11:30 so they could arrive at the field house in time for the meeting. When they arrived, Rockwell and Corrigan were standing in the front of the room. Corrigan counted heads and nodded to Rockwell. "They're all here, except Dean, Sparks, and Diston."

Rockwell picked up a sheaf of papers from the desk and walked to the center of the room. "Men," he said, "I've just come from Dean Murray's office. And I've got some bad news.

"First, Diston, Dean, and Sparks are ineligible because of academic difficulties. That's a disastrous blow to our pitching hopes. Second, the papers Jim is going to hand out have been approved by Dean Murray. They'll be filed in his office after you sign them.

"It all boils down to one simple point. Every player in this room who signs the pledge in good faith will be permitted to play baseball for State. Those who do not sign are to be dropped from the squad."

Corrigan had passed out the papers while Rockwell was talking. When he finished, he rejoined Rockwell in the front of the room.

PAY-OFF PITCH

Date: _____
To: Dean Walter Murray
From:
Subject: Job held last summer and baseball played.
(Please fill out the following spaces with perti-
nent information. If additional space is required,
use the back of this form. Please be accurate;
this information will be confirmed immediately.)

Full Name: _____
Home Address: _____
Home Telephone: _____ /
University Address: _____
Telephone: _____
Class: _____

I hereby certify that I spent the past summer in
_____ (which covers the entire
period from the time I left University on May 20 or there-
abouts until the first day of school last August).
Name of employer: _____
Address: _____
Name of baseball team or teams of which I was a member: _____

I hereby certify that I did not receive pay or any kind of
remuneration for playing baseball last summer or at any
other time. I further certify that I am not under contract
to play professional baseball and that I have never been
under such a contract or agreement.
Signed: _____

There was a stunned silence after the players had
time to read the form and absorb the implications. Then
an angry murmur began in the back row where Widow
Wilder was sitting with his buddies.

A LIFE TURNED AROUND

"What's the trouble?" Rockwell asked.

"You ought to know," Wilder said rebelliously, getting slowly to his feet. "This is your idea, isn't it?"

"Partly," Rockwell said coolly. "Why?"

"Well, how would you feel if you were in our place and asked to sign this piece of nonsense?" Wilder crumpled the paper in his hand and remained standing, glaring at Rockwell.

"Not too bad," Rockwell said quietly. "In fact, when I was a student here at State, I signed the same kind of a form."

"Well, I won't!" Wilder snapped, throwing the crumpled form across the room. He glanced at his friends and stalked toward the door. "I quit!"

There was an instant of hesitation, and then Al Engle, Lee Carter, George Reed, and the two Harris brothers got to their feet and followed Wilder. At the door, Engle turned and glared at Dugan. "You coming, Doogie?"

CHAPTER 13

Off the Team

DOOGIE DUGAN hadn't moved. Then, to the surprise of everyone in the room, he shook his head firmly. "No, Al," he said clearly. "I'm not coming. I want to play ball."

Engle's jaw slackened. "What?" he declared, staring in disbelief at his pal. "OK," he said finally, shrugging his broad shoulders. "I'll see you later."

When the rebellious group slammed out the door, Rockwell faced the remaining players and nodded grimly. "All right, men, if any of you have questions, ask them. If not, sign the form and dress for the game." Corrigan moved down the aisle and collected the papers. Then one by one, the players left the room.

Chip didn't have much to write on his form. He filled it out completely, certifying that he had not played baseball the previous summer. He listed the details of his job at Camp All-America and added that he had played in several pickup games with the campers and members of the staff. When he finished the form, he followed the other players down the steps to the locker room.

Surprisingly, Wilder's action had not brought the relief Chip had expected. He felt sad and depressed. He tried to tell himself that Wilder had made the decision and he could now forget all about it and concentrate on baseball. But it didn't help.

Chip waited until Soapy had suited up. They left the locker room together. Speed, Biggie, Fireball, and Schwartz followed. Chip was thinking about the game and scarcely noticed several players and students standing beside the parking lot fence, but a protesting voice drew his attention. He looked more carefully at the group. Al Engle had Doogie Dugan up against the fence, and Widow Wilder and several curious spectators were watching. The two junior college friends were arguing heatedly.

"I'm not going to do it, Al," Dugan said stubbornly. "I want to play."

"All right then, play!" Engle said angrily. He reached out suddenly, caught Doogie by the throat, and shoved him roughly back against the wire. Then he banged the little pitcher's head against the wire fence several times.

"Hey, hold it!" Chip cried, leaping forward and pulling Engle away from Dugan. "What are you trying to do?"

Engle whirled around and faced Chip. "What's it to you?" he rasped. "Keep your hands to yourself."

"Why don't you try that?" Chip retorted. "Doogie's your friend, Al. Come on, forget it. That's no way to settle a difference of opinion."

"Maybe you'd like to settle it," Wilder snarled, shoving Engle aside and facing Chip. "Your way is to sneak behind a guy's back and run to the coach and tell him a pack of lies. Right?"

"I'm not trying to settle anything," Chip said quietly. "But that's not the point. Dugan is only half as big as Engle."

"You're more than half my size," Wilder said angrily. "If you don't like it, why don't you do something about it? With me!"

"No," Chip said quietly. He turned away and glanced at Dugan. "Coming with us?"

Dugan hesitated and glanced at Engle. But his former pal's expression was hard and unrelenting. The little pitcher shook his head in resignation. "Yeah," he said. "I'm coming with you guys."

Biggie, Soapy, Speed, Red, and Fireball had ringed the Wilder group without being noticed. They joined Chip and Dugan and walked slowly toward the diamond. Behind them, Wilder and Engle muttered something about quitters and snitchers.

"I don't know what's wrong with Al," Dugan said dejectedly. "He hasn't been the same since he started hanging around with Wilder. Man, we've been friends for years."

"He'll get over it," Chip said.

"I don't know. I've never seen him like this. I don't want to have any trouble with Al, but I can't see quitting baseball just because the coach asked me to sign a little piece of paper."

"It stands for a lot."

"Lots of little pieces of paper stand for a lot," Dugan breathed quietly.

When they reached the dugout, the Poly Tech players were warming up on the other side of the field. Rockwell waited patiently until his players circled him before giving instructions. "We'll hit in this order," he said. "Merton, Minson, Bentley, Cohen, Finley, Ryder, Burke, Smith, and Rickard. Soapy, you warm up Hex. Nickels, take care of Chip and Dugan. Crowell, you throw to the hitters. The rest of you do the fielding."

Chip and Dugan said nothing as they alternated throws to Nickels. Each was busy with his own thoughts. Chip was thinking about Wilder and all the trouble the braggart had caused. The same depression gripping Chip seemed to descend on the rest of the players.

Soapy and Ozzie Crowell tried to shake their team-mates out of it, but they didn't get anywhere. And when the Statesmen took the field to face the Tech hitters in the first inning, they looked like a beaten team. All the pep, spirit, and confidence that mark a good team were missing. But the fans greeted Rickard enthusiastically when he walked out to the mound. Now this was better! And when they saw Biggie on first base and Fireball out in center field, their spirits picked up and they got solidly behind the team.

Rickard pitched a good game. He put everything he had into his throws and struck out nine hitters. Soapy caught the first five innings and Nickels the last four. Hex allowed only six hits, but jittery support and several bad throws resulted in six runs for the Engineers.

Biggie and Fireball each got three for four, but the Tech pitcher handcuffed the rest of the State hitters. The result was three runs. The Tech hurler had started shakily, but as each inning passed and the legendary slugging power of the Statesmen was arrested, he became more sure of himself. Now in the bottom of the ninth, with Tech leading 6-3, he was supremely confident.

Chip was hoping for a chance to hit, and he got it. Rockwell turned to the dugout. "Crowell," he called, "hit for Burke. Durley for Nickels. Hilton for Rickard. Smith, warm up Dugan. All right, it's never too late! Let's go get this ball game."

PAY-OFF PITCH

Ozzie "The Whiz" Crowell was one of the smallest players on the squad. And when he crouched over the plate, his personal strike zone appeared only a little larger than home plate. Ozzie was up there for one purpose and one purpose only: to get on base at any cost. He worked the pitcher to two and no, two and one, three and one, three and two, and finally to ball four. So the Whiz was on first with no one down.

Andre Durley was grimly determined. He didn't like to sit in the dugout and watch a ball game. He took a strike, looked at a ball, and then slammed an outside pitch into right field. Crowell went all the way to third, and Durley held up at second base. That brought Chip up with no one down and two ducks on the pond.

The fans were in a frenzy now, imploring Chip to get a piece of the ball. Chip did just that, catching a fastball with the sweet spot of his bat. The ball took off for the left-field fence. It banged up against the fence and rebounded into the field with the Tech left and center fielders in hot pursuit.

As soon as his bat met the ball, Chip knew he had tagged it! He sprinted as hard as he could around first, made the turn at second, and was halfway to third base when the left fielder got the ball. A year ago, Chip could have stretched that hit into a home run. But not now. His leg slowed him up. He made the third-base turn but had to double back when the throw came in hard and sure and straight for the plate. So there he was on third base, carrying the tying run with no one down, and with State's heavy end of the stick at bat.

Chip glanced at Minson. He knew Coach Rockwell wanted that run, knew that he wouldn't want to take a chance on losing the tying tally. Then Chip got the sign. The squeeze was on.

OFF THE TEAM

The first pitch was high, and Minson watched it go by. But the next one was in there, and Minson tried to lay it down. The result was a weak pop-up the catcher took and then fired back to third for the double-play attempt. Chip was forced to slide and barely got back in time. That brought up Bill Bentley. Chip watched the husky fielder closely. This time the sign showed that Bentley was on his own; he could hit away.

Bentley went for the first pitch and caught it right on the nose. The ball took off on a slow-rising line over first base. The fans rose en masse, cheering wildly.

Their cheers subsided as quickly.

The Tech first baseman leaped high in the air and speared the liner. Then he fired a hard clothesline peg across the infield to third base. This time, Chip was caught.

He had started for home, but when he saw the catch, he tried to get back to the base. He made a desperate slide, but he was too late. The ball beat him to the bag for the double play, and the game was over. The score: Poly Tech 6, State 5.

As soon as Chip heard the base umpire call him out, he started for the field house. "I lost it!" he muttered. "Stupid base-running."

Soapy came running up with his jacket and his glove. "Too bad, Chipper."

"I'll say it is," Chip said bitterly. "What a stupid play."

"You can say that again," someone drawled behind him.

Chip turned in the direction of the voice. Widow Wilder and Al Engle, standing shoulder to shoulder, smirked at Chip's play.

"Some base-running," Engle mocked. "I've seen Little League kids who could do better than that."

"Yeah," Wilder agreed mockingly. "But you forgot something, Al. Hilton has to be the hero. Or didn't you know?"

Soapy was burning. "You guys quit. Why don't you get out of here?" he challenged angrily. "Why don't you two idiots grow up?"

"Come on, Soapy," Chip urged. "Don't waste your time."

Soapy was up early the next morning. He shook Chip's shoulder gently. "Want the papers, Chip?"

"Nope," said Chip. "Can't be anything except bad news."

"Well, we might as well read it," Soapy replied. "I sure heard enough bad news last night. Seemed like every guy who wanted a Coke had to make a snide comment.

"One guy would say, 'We can't win for losing.' Another would say, 'I think it's the coach.' And another, 'Man, that freshman team was overrated. They won't help the varsity.' Then, 'Where was Wilder?' Another jerk, 'Yeah, this was our year to win the conference, right!'

"And you know something, Chip? Every one of those guys looked straight at me while he was talking." Soapy snorted in disgust. "Some fun. I'll be back in a couple minutes."

Chip groaned and got up. Once Soapy got started with his Sunday morning newspaper research, sleep was impossible. He was dressed and checking his E-mail when Soapy returned.

"Here's the bad news," Soapy announced. "Let's read Jim Locke's column first."

He opened the *News* to the sports page and glanced at the headlines. "Hey, Chip! Look at this! Look at this headline."

OFF THE TEAM

Soapy held the paper up in front of Chip's eyes and jabbed his finger at the headline. "Look at that!"

**STATE BASEBALL CAPTAIN EXPOSED AND
DROPPED FROM VARSITY BASEBALL TEAM**
Mitch "Widow" Wilder
Played Professional Ball

"How about that!" Soapy gasped.

CHAPTER 14

Soaring Spirits

WIDOW WILDER picked up his suitcases and glanced around his dorm room. "I guess that's it," he said. "Be sure to UPS my stereo and these boxes first thing in the morning."

"Don't worry about it," Engle said. "It's as good as done, man."

"Let's go," Wilder said shortly. "I'll be glad to get on that bus and out of this town."

"I sure hate to see you quit school, Mitch," Engle said. "But I promise one thing—I'll take care of Hilton for you."

"How?"

"I don't know, but I will."

"There's only one way," Wilder mused. "It's got to be through baseball. You'll have to get back on the team."

"You mean crawl back?"

"Why not? What do you care?"

"Well, if that's the only way—"

SOARING SPIRITS

Just about that time, Chip and Soapy were setting out for church. They walked slowly across the campus and took the shortcut down Coach Rockwell's street, enjoying the sunny morning.

"Oh, oh," Soapy whispered anxiously as he elbowed Chip. He nodded ahead. "Trouble."

Widow Wilder and Al Engle were standing on the corner. Two suitcases were on the sidewalk beside Wilder. It was too late to avoid them, so Chip and Soapy continued until they reached the corner. As they approached, Wilder and Engle turned to face them.

Chip nodded and spoke. "Hey, Wilder, Engle."

Mitch Wilder grunted and stepped directly into Chip's path, blocking his way. His eyes glittered and his jaw hardened. "I *would* run into you," he said bitterly. "You must feel pretty proud of yourself, betraying a guy who was trying to do you a favor. You know something? I almost believed you when you fed me all that stuff about playing fair and being loyal to your teammates and the school and your friends."

"Sure," Engle broke in angrily, "but then he turned around and ran to the coach with a lot of lies."

"That's right," Wilder added menacingly. "I saw you myself. I saw you come sneaking out of Rockwell's house like some kind of snake slithering out from under a rock. You and Rockwell cooked up that pledge idea together, didn't you? Just to get me."

Chip was surprised by the sudden attack. The injustice of the accusations struck him hard. While he tried to collect his thoughts, the smoldering anger that had been burning in his heart during the troublesome days caught fire in a torrent of words.

"That's a lie. I never snitched on anyone in my life. And you weren't doing *me* any favor, Wilder. Don't kid yourself. Your idea of loyalty is like a one-way street. All one way. Your way! What kind of honesty and loyalty do you call playing summer ball for money? With all your baseball experience, you never learned the first principles of sportsmanship or loyalty or what sports stand for. And until you do, you'll never be a major-leaguer. A man's good name is *everything*. He doesn't try to shield it by playing under an assumed name like a coward."

Wilder's face contorted in sudden, uncontrollable rage. "You can't call me a coward!" he shouted. "You—you quitter! You sneak." He bounded forward and launched a wild swing at Chip's head.

The punch never landed. Soapy moved in like a streak, caught the outflung arm, and whirled Wilder around and away from Chip. "Oh, no you don't!" he gasped.

Engle just stood there watching, but after Soapy's cry, he jumped into action. He caught Soapy from behind with a ferocious blow to his head and then maneuvered in front of his stunned opponent to deliver a right hook that fully connected with Soapy's jaw. Soapy fell to one knee and then came back to his feet with a rush.

"Hold it!" Chip shouted. "Hold it, Engle! This concerns Wilder and me."

"I'll say," Wilder snarled, pulling Engle to one side. "Come on, Hilton. We'll settle this for good." He wrestled out of his jacket, muttering angrily.

"Don't do it, Chip," Soapy cried. "He won't fight fair! Besides, he outweighs you by forty pounds."

"I'm not worried about that," Chip said, pulling off his sweater. Then he regained his senses. He was suddenly ashamed of his lack of control and disgusted by the scene: a fight just like drunks outside a bar. On Sunday. And on the way to church.

"Wait a minute, Wilder," Chip said, dropping his arms. "This is stupid. A fight's not going to settle anything." He stepped back and eyed Wilder steadily. "I didn't want any part of this. You started it. Someday you'll find out the truth. All I want to say is that I didn't write any notes, and I never mentioned your name to Coach Rockwell."

"That's what you say," Wilder sneered bitterly. "But it had to be you."

"I'm sorry, Wilder," Chip said slowly. "I'm sorry you're leaving school, and I'm sorry we can't part as friends. Come on, Soapy."

"Let him go, Mitch," Engle said contemptuously. "I always knew he was yellow."

Chip nearly lost his control then. But he shook off the angry urge and walked away. Soapy was about as angry as Chip had ever seen him in all the years they had been friends. They continued down the street while Wilder and Engle hurled angry insults after them.

When Chip and Soapy returned from church, their friends had taken over their room and were listening to the stereo, reading the papers, and talking about Widow Wilder. They greeted Chip and Soapy excitedly.

"Hear about Wilder?" Speed asked excitedly.

"We read it," Chip said. "It's too bad."

"Good riddance in my opinion," Biggie growled.

"I'm sorry to see him leave school," Chip said.

"He needs more than school," Soapy said bitterly.

"Anyway," Fireball said, "things will be different now."

Things *were* different Monday afternoon when the players reported for practice. There was a new atmosphere in the locker room and in the way the players talked and joked with one another. And out on the field, everyone seemed to be straining at the leash, impatient to forget the defeats and the cliques and the hard feelings.

The new spirit gripped Rockwell too. He was his old self, pepping up the practice and driving the players at top speed through the calisthenics, fielding, hitting, and running. And it was the same in the stands. Scattered groups of students and fans were watching the practice and talking about Widow Wilder, Henry Rockwell, and the players. Their comments were all optimistic. All expressed new confidence and a cocky "watch 'em go now!" air.

Midway through the practice, Chip and Hex were throwing to Soapy in front of the dugout, loosening up their arms. Rockwell stood nearby, watching the hitters. Chip felt great. His arm was strong, and he was finally able to concentrate on the target offered by Soapy's big glove. He reared back and burned one into Soapy's mitt with a grunt of satisfaction.

Soapy let the ball smack full into the pocket of his glove, and the resulting sound was like the crack of a gun. "Yahoo!" Soapy yelled. "Yow!" Then the happy catcher held the ball in his hand and motioned almost imperceptibly toward Rockwell. Chip and Hex both turned and were surprised to see Al Engle approaching the coach.

Engle was dressed in jeans and a sweatshirt, and he was openly carrying a piece of paper in his hand. Chip and Hex immediately resumed their throwing, but it was impossible not to hear the conversation between the surly catcher and Rockwell.

"Hello, Engle," Rockwell said.

Engle ignored the salutation. "Is it too late for me to sign the paper?" he asked abruptly. "Too late to come back?"

SOARING SPIRITS

"No, of course not."

"Here it is, and it's signed. It was my mistake."

A number of spectators in the bleachers saw Al Engle shake hands with Rockwell. One of them was particularly interested. He waited until Engle came trotting back to the field in uniform. Then, when Rockwell called the squad into the dugout, he got to his feet and slowly made his way down to the field.

Just as the tall man reached the gate leading to the dugout, Rockwell saw him and pushed his way through the circle of players. "Del!" he cried. "This is a welcome surprise." He turned to the players. "Look who's here!"

Coach Del Bennett smiled and motioned for silence. "Hi, men. I guess you're wondering why I'm here. Well, I've been reading about your troubles. I guess I should say Coach Rockwell's troubles. Anyway, I've heard all about it from a number of sources. Like you, I'm glad it's over. Now you can get together and play a little baseball."

"Now that you're back, we will," Rockwell said.

"Hold it, Rock," Bennett interrupted. "I'm not back. And I won't be back. This season anyway. The gallbladder was just the beginning. The old ticker isn't in the best of shape. My doctor has ordered a complete rest." He shook his head wryly. "Nope, I'll have to do my coaching from the stands."

There was a short, awkward silence. Then Rockwell voiced everyone's feelings. "We're sorry to hear that, Del. It's a tough break for you and the team. But we want you to know, we'll be playing for you. This is *your* ball club, and we're going to make you proud of it."

Rockwell's words voiced the sentiments of the players. They roared their approval.

"Absolutely!"

"Say that again!"

PAY-OFF PITCH

"We'll move now!"

Rockwell held up his hand for silence. "All right, team. One more thing. We'll elect a captain to replace Wilder just before the Wilson University game."

Al Engle was the only one of Wilder's crew to report back for the team. And it was just as well. Biggie Cohen overshadowed Reggie Harris at first base like a giant tree over a seedling. Lenny Harris was a fair pitcher, but he had no chance to win a starting assignment in competition with Chip and Rickard. And in center field, Fireball Finley had moved in solid. George Reed didn't have a chance.

When the Statesmen left for the Southern University game Wednesday night, the players acted more like a championship ball club than a team that had lost four straight games. And the next afternoon, they performed like champions. Chip started on the mound and went all the way, striking out eleven of the Southerners and allowing only four hits for a shutout victory. The State batters came to life, too, touching three rival pitchers for a total of twelve hits and nine runs and giving State its first win of the season. The score: State 9, Southern 0.

On Friday, back home for the Western game, Rickard pitched magnificently, giving up six well-scattered hits and keeping the visitors scoreless. The State hitters were still on a hitting spree and slugged in eight runs. It was the second shutout in a row, and the spirits of every player on the squad rose. The score: State 8, Western 0.

Saturday brought the A & M game, and University was filled with excitement. In every conference and in every league, there are two or more teams that because of geographic location, championship contention, or some sort of feud develop and maintain a keen rivalry. Such a rivalry existed between State and A & M. The two schools usually battled for the conference lead in all sports. And when an outsider won, it was usually Southwestern. Next to A & M, Southwestern rated second as the team State liked best to defeat.

On Saturday, the fans flocked to Alumni Field to see the battle. The Aggies had a lot of supporters in the stands too. They were seated behind the visitors' dugout and kept up a steady chatter of encouragement for their team while also throwing out a few taunts and challenges for the State players and fans.

Dugan started on the mound with Nickels behind the plate, Russ Merton at shortstop, Biggie on first base, Ozzie Crowell on second; Jaime "Minnie" Minson held down the hot corner. The outfield lined up with Bentley in left, Fireball in center, and Ellis "Belter" Burke in right.

The Aggies got to Dugan in the very first inning, scoring three runs on a walk and three straight hits. In their half of the inning, the Statesmen led off with Merton, Minson, and Bentley. Merton walked, Minson grounded out, advancing Merton to second, and Bill Bentley lifted a high fly to right field. That brought Biggie up with Merton still perched on second base.

Then Biggie, batting lefty, brought the home fans to their feet by lifting a fastball pitch high and far toward the right-field fence. The ball kept going, on and on and on. That ball was gone! The crowd roared its approval. Merton took it easy coming in, and Biggie was practically on his heels when they crossed the plate with two runs for State.

The cheers for Biggie had scarcely died away when Fireball repeated the performance. But Fireball's hit was different. It took off like a missile and headed straight for the left-field fence. And it was still rising when it cleared the barrier. It was a home run in any league. Ozzie Crowell flied out, but the score was all tied up at three runs each.

That was the way the game went. The A & M Aggies could hit and they could field. So could the Statesmen. Rockwell replaced Dugan and Nickels with Chip and Engle in the top of the seventh with two down, the bases loaded, and the score tied 9-9.

The cleanup hitter was at bat, and he was dangerous. Chip pitched too carefully, and with the count at three and two, he tried to catch the inside corner. But the husky hitter stepped into the pitch and laced a screaming liner over the left-field fence. The Aggies fans went berserk as four runs crossed the plate. The next hitter grounded out, and A & M was out in front 13-9 in the top of the seventh.

Chip walked slowly off the field, disappointed and disgusted. Before he reached the dugout, Engle caught up with him. "You sure blew that hero spot, Hilton," he whispered slyly.

Chip was caught by surprise. Before he could reply, Engle walked quickly over to the bat rack.

CHAPTER 15

Inside-the-Park Homer

A GRAND-SLAM HOMER does more than score four runs. It gives the team at bat confidence, and it often demoralizes the other club. But the Statesmen were far from demoralized. A week earlier, they might have folded. But today the Statesmen were a fighting team led by a fighting coach.

Henry Rockwell's integrity and patient coaching methods had won his players' respect. He had demonstrated that he believed in every player on the squad, whether the player was on the field or on the bench. And he had demonstrated that he wasn't afraid to use his players in a game—any of them.

Belter Burke was up at bat with Crowell on deck and Engle in the hole. Burke lifted a high fly to left field for an easy out, Crowell grounded out, and Engle went down swinging.

Chip couldn't shake Engle's surprise verbal attack from his mind. Nobody else had heard Al's comment, and his performance behind the plate gave no evidence of anything but the perfect relationship expected of team-mates. Engle took a little time getting together his catching gear, so Chip warmed up with Soapy. Then Engle took the glove from Soapy, and the batter stepped up to the plate.

Chip was still upset and walked the first hitter. The next batter hit a sharp ground ball to Minson's right, but Minnie made the stop and fired the ball to Merton in time to get the runner. Merton pivoted, and his throw to Biggie beat the walked batter by a whisker. The double play settled Chip down, and he struck out the next hitter.

Chip led off for State in the next round and worked the pitcher for a walk. Merton flied out, and Chip was held at first. Minson singled to right, advancing Chip to third. And when Bentley doubled to right field, Chip scored. Minson held up at third. Biggie tossed away two extra bats and moved into the lefty's batting box with a chance to tie up the game.

Biggie hit the first pitch. But he was late, and his swing was hurried. The result was a line drive straight into the third baseman's glove. The alert baseman raced to the bag and beat Minson by a hair to complete the solo double play. Chip's run had made the score: State 10, A & M 13.

Chip had settled down now, put Engle out of his thoughts, and was back in form for the ninth. He struck out the first two batters and forced the third hitter to lift a high foul along the first-base line that Biggie pulled in for the third out. When State came in for its last licks, Fireball was up, Burke was on deck, and Crowell was in the hole.

Right then, Rockwell took a desperate chance. He sent Red Schwartz in to bat for Fireball, Soapy for

Burke, and Speed for Crowell. Chip held his breath. Henry Rockwell had always made it tough for his former high school players—had always left it up to them to make their own breaks. Now he was placing them in the toughest spot possible.

Schwartz stood an even six feet and weighed 180 pounds. He was as hard as a rock and he could give the ball a ride. Red gave the ball a ride now, smashing a Texas leaguer over third base that rolled clear to the left-field corner. He pulled up at second base. Soapy looked at two balls and then shot a sizzling grounder past third base. Schwartz was held at third, and Soapy stopped at first. Speed Morris came to the plate with a chance to tie up the game!

The Aggies infielders moved in on the grass to cut off the run at the plate. It looked as if the squeeze play was on when Speed bunted. But it was only a fake! Schwartz started in far enough to secure attention as Speed beat out the bunt, moving Soapy to second base. The ducks were on the pond! That brought up Engle.

Engle took his time getting to the plate. There, standing just outside the batting box, he put on a big show, knocking at his spikes with his bat, tugging on his batting helmet, and rubbing his hands on his pants. Then he stepped into the box and got set.

The Aggies pitcher blazed in a fastball, and Engle cut at it with all his power. It was an outside pitch and made the burly catcher look bad, even though he got a piece of the ball. The result was a high foul ball that the catcher pulled in easily for the out.

Chip had a tight feeling around his chest. Now it was up to him. Then he saw Engle walking back from first base, swinging his head in disgust. "All right, Al, old boy," he whispered to himself, "now we'll see about that hero spot."

PAY-OFF PITCH

The fans were in a frenzy. This was a storybook setting! The home team was behind, 10-13, playing its most bitter rival; it was the bottom of the ninth, the bases were loaded, and Hilton was up with a chance to win his own game.

The crowd gave Chip a tremendous ovation as he walked across to the first-base side of the plate. Before the pitcher could toe the rubber, however, the A & M coach called time and walked out to the mound for a conference.

Chip breathed a sigh of relief and stepped back out of the box. He knocked the dirt out of his spikes with the bat and glanced around the bases. His Valley Falls hometown teammates were on the bases; the situation brought back a lot of memories. He had been in this kind of a spot before, but that had been high school baseball, and he and his pals had been regulars. This was different. This was NCAA baseball, and he, Red, Speed, Biggie, and Soapy were newcomers. Besides, A & M was State's most bitter rival. The fans would never forgive him if he failed now.

The A & M coach walked back to the dugout, and Chip stepped into the box. He looked at the first pitch, a low, fast one that came in around the knees for a called strike. The Aggies pitcher kept the next one close, too, but it missed the corner for ball one. The next pitch was low and outside for another ball; the count was two and one. "So that's it," Chip breathed. "They're going to keep everything low."

Chip was ahead of the pitcher now, and he set himself for another low pitch. He was right—the ball came in just above the knees, and Chip went for it. The crack of the bat was sharp and clear and rang with authority. The blow turned Chip toward first in full stride, and he saw the ball land beyond second base and head for right-center field.

Speed was nearly to second base, Soapy was on his way to third, and Red was yelling behind Chip, already home. Chip cut loose at top speed, his long legs eating up the dirt. Chip forgot his knee and everything else except the desire to stretch the hit as far as possible. As he rounded second, he saw Coach Corrigan waving him on from the third-base coaching box. He turned his head toward the center fielder and saw him pick up the ball. The second baseman was moving out for the cutoff.

Corrigan was waving him on, his arm windmilling vigorously as he urged Chip on by moving toward home plate. Chip made the turn around third and looked for the cutoff player. At the same time he looked for the ball. "It's too high!" he gasped. "It's over his head. I can make it!"

One last glance caught the pitcher backing up and extending his glove for the ball. "It's going to be close," Chip muttered, calling on every ounce of his strength.

The crowd roar was booming out and around him as he concentrated on the catcher. Up ahead, the burly receiver held his glove low, and Chip knew the ball was coming in on a low, perfect bounce. Chip took off in a hard hook slide under the catcher, just as the ball arrived. He and the catcher crashed to the ground, but Chip's long right leg hit the plate. The dust obscured his vision, but a split second later, he heard the umpire bellow, "Safe!" and saw the ball lying near the plate.

It was a grand-slam blow on an inside-the-park homer! The game was over, and the Statesmen had won the big game with their archrival and registered their third-straight win! The score: State 14, A & M 13.

PAY-OFF PITCH

Soapy was awake early. Barefoot, he bounded down the stairs two at a time to grab a paper from each of the stacks on the front porch of Jefferson Hall. This time, Chip could hardly wait for the redhead to return. He didn't have long to wait. Soapy came bustling back, grinning from ear to ear and carrying a copy of the *News* open to the sports pages.

"Listen!" he demanded, bursting through the door. "Listen to this headline. Quote! 'Hilton's inside-the-park home run wins it for State.'"

Soapy tossed the *News* to Chip and buried his nose in the *Herald*.

Chip read the story of the game and studied the box score. It was a big victory, all right. Any victory over A & M was a big one.

"That was A & M's first defeat, Chip. Did you know that?"

"Sure."

"Makes us look pretty good, doesn't it?" Soapy grinned widely. "They win eight in a row, and then we knock 'em off. Guess you saw the conference standing?"

"Nope."

"Well, Southwestern is on top with ten straight. They haven't lost yet. A & M is in second place with eight and one, thanks to us, and Brandon is in third place." He grunted and continued. "You know where we are?"

"I can guess," Chip answered wryly.

"You're right. Last place."

"We'll take care of that before long."

"You can say that again. Hey, here's a picture of Hex Rickard! Big story too. Listen! 'Hector "Hex" Rickard has a flair for baseball and science—in either order—and is currently making news in two important places. As a baseball player, the six-foot-180-pound senior is being mentioned prominently by those who pick all-American teams.'"

Soapy looked at Chip and nodded his head. "So right, eh?"

"No question about it."

"Now listen to this—"

"I'm listening."

"'As a chemical engineering student, Rickard is being observed closely by an outfit called Phi Beta Kappa. The State University southpaw is a good example of a talented athletic student who excels in the classroom and on the diamond. The popular senior defrays part of his college expenses (fourth-straight year) by working in the laboratory of the Burns Wells Company, a local research engineering organization, twenty hours per week. Rickard has never made less than an A in any class during his four years of study.'"

Soapy paused. "Are you listening?"

"I certainly am."

"Well, let's see. Here it is. 'The portsider confesses that he loves baseball, but he insists that his life's work comes first and that his last game will be in a State uniform.'" Soapy paused again. "Imagine! He's gonna quit baseball."

"That's why we're going to elect him captain of the team," Chip said softly.

"But he doesn't want the job," Soapy protested. "He said you were a natural leader. Look, Chip. He was the first guy to sign the paper to elect you. And—"

"I know," Chip interrupted. "He's the kind of man who boosts everyone but himself. You and I are going to work for *him*."

"But I don't see—"

"I do. Who else do you know who works while he's going to school, turned down a big-league baseball contract, makes excellent grades, and demonstrates such sportsmanship? Name one guy."

Soapy grinned. "That's easy. Chip Hilton!"

Chip fired the *Herald* at Soapy and started for the shower. At the door he turned and pointed a threatening finger at his pal. "We're voting for Hex Rickard, right?"

"Right, Chip," Soapy said, grinning. "We'll settle for the next two years."

Chip and Soapy campaigned feverishly on Monday and Tuesday. And when Henry Rockwell called for the election of a captain just before the Wilson University game on Wednesday, Rickard was unanimously elected captain. Then the Statesmen went out and beat the visitors, 7-2.

Chip pitched seven innings, and State led 4-0 when Doogie Dugan came in to replace him. He was wild but managed to finish the game. Once more, Rockwell used practically every player on the squad, and it was obvious there were no subs on this team.

The Statesmen were really on their way now. That weekend they journeyed to Brandon for a two-game series on Friday and Saturday. State won the first, 6-5, and they were leading in the second, 7-2, when rain stopped that game in the fourth inning.

The following week, they beat Eastern once and Northern State twice, bringing their tally to eight straight wins. It was a fighting, hustling team now, and the fans woke up to the fact that State had a strong ball club.

During the next two weeks, they streaked by Templeton, swamped Midwestern twice, beat Brandon to tie for third place in the conference, whitewashed Northern State, and capped the brilliant streak by taking a twin bill from Southeastern for their fifteenth-straight win.

State's baseball team had practically pushed all other news off the sports page with their exciting winning streak.

That Sunday morning it seemed to Chip that Soapy was up at daylight. And when he came back upstairs with the Sunday papers, the exuberant redhead was so pleased he was walking on air. Chip could hear him reading aloud all the way up the steps and along the hall. And when he burst into the room, he kept right on talking.

"Says here in the *News* . . . Hey! You listening?"

"How could I help it?"

"It says—now listen! 'State baseball team wins number fifteen!' That's the headline. Now get this: 'After losing the first four games, State's one-two punch of Hector Rickard and Chip Hilton has carried the Statesmen to fifteen consecutive victories.' Not bad, huh?

"'Only in college baseball could two pitchers carry an entire schedule on their backs. However, it so happens that these are not ordinary pitchers. Chip Hilton has won eight games in a row without a defeat.'" Soapy stopped long enough to catch his breath and smile at his roommate. "That's what I call superduper publicity, Chip, but there's even more!

"'Captain Hex Rickard has won seven in a row; his pitching record is marred only by a single early-season defeat. As further evidence of the effectiveness of Hilton and Rickard, Doogie Dugan, the pint-sized junior college relief pitcher, has yet to be called upon to come to the rescue of Rockwell's two aces.

"'The locals are now firmly entrenched in third place with a record of fifteen wins and four losses. Just a step ahead, A & M is occupying second place with a record of sixteen victories and four defeats. Southwestern is in undisputed possession of first place with a record of eighteen wins and two losses with four games still left to play.'" Soapy whistled in admiration. "How about those guys!"

"They must be pretty good. Anything else?"

"Well, let's see now. Yes! Here it is. 'The Statesmen have five more conference games to play. It is not beyond the realm of possibility that they will win them all.'"

Soapy grunted. "Possibility? It's a cinch! Hmmm. 'Continuing along this line, it is also possible that Southwestern might lose two of its remaining games. In this event, the upcoming home contest between State and Southwestern could decide the conference championship.'"

CHAPTER 16

Lightning Strikes Twice

THE PRESSURE was on! Every player, every student, and every fan in University knew that State's baseball team had a good chance to beat out A & M for the runner-up spot and a slim chance to win the conference championship. The *News* and the *Herald* featured the battle between State and A & M for second place as well as carrying the conference standings on the sports pages every day.

The Statesmen kept up the pace—they kept right on winning. On Wednesday they blasted Cathedral out of the park with a score of 14-3 to avenge their earlier loss, and the win brought their season record to sixteen victories and four defeats. Thursday night, when they headed for Brandon, the Statesmen and A & M were tied for second place. State's players were happy and confident and enjoyed the ride, joking and laughing and living up to the old axiom that a happy club is a winning club.

On the bus Chip did some reading and then went back to sit with Speed. When the team arrived in

Brandon and checked into the hotel, Chip immediately went to bed. Rockwell let the players sleep late, ordering a team brunch for eleven o'clock. At one o'clock, their bus took them to Brandon's campus, where they dressed for the game.

When they got to the field, they had it all to themselves. Rockwell put them through a long hitting practice; they had only their infield drills to get out of the way when the Brandon players arrived.

Brandon was doomed for fourth place in the conference but played as if it was battling for the championship. The Brandon pitcher was right, and so was Rickard. The game developed into a pitchers' duel. Neither team scored until the Statesmen came to bat in the top of the seventh.

Darrin Nickels walked, and Rickard advanced him to second base with a sacrifice bunt. Minson singled sharply to left field, and Nickels hustled to third base. Then Rockwell flashed the sign to Corrigan in the coaching box. The squeeze was on!

Merton was an expert push-along artist. On the second pitch he tapped a slow roller along the third-base line. Nickels and the Brandon third baseman came tearing in together. The infielder played the ball perfectly, scooping it up and pegging it to the catcher in a single motion. The ball and Nickels converged on the catcher simultaneously, but the big Statesman beat the tag by a hair and slid across the plate for the first run of the game.

The State players cheered the play but sobered quickly when Nickels did not get up. Rockwell raced out to the plate, and the Brandon team physician reached Nickels a few seconds later. He made a quick examination and called for a stretcher. "Hip!" he said shortly. "Dislocated. I'll take him to the hospital."

LIGHTNING STRIKES TWICE

Darrin's teammates crowded around him while they waited for the ambulance. And when the trainers carried him away on a stretcher, the big sophomore grinned broadly and said, "I guess I'll have to sit this one out. Go get 'em, guys!"

Fireball struck out, and Biggie lifted a long, high fly for the third out. Engle replaced Nickels behind the plate when the Statesmen took the field. Suddenly, just as it happens again and again in sports, a streak of bad luck followed. Ground-ball errors, wild throws, and misjudged flies plagued the Statesmen and resulted in a victory for Brandon, 6-1. The defeat broke State's consecutive victory streak and gave the Statesmen a season record of sixteen and five.

After the game, Rockwell hustled them in and out of the locker room and onto their bus to return to University. They stopped for dinner along the way, pulling up in front of the State University field house late than night. Clapping each player on the back as he climbed down off the bus, Rock told his team to get some sleep and be ready for the next afternoon's game with A & M, the first of the vital two-game series.

Even before the Statesmen reached University, they learned that A & M had won its game with Wilson University to give the Aggies a record of seventeen and four, moving them into second place in the conference.

Chip, Soapy, and Biggie piled into Speed's Mustang, and Red hopped into the front passenger seat of Fireball's old yellow Volkswagen. Both carloads went straight home to Jeff. They were quietly determined. The next two games had to be won. "Well take 'em," Soapy said confidently. "Rock will use Chip, and he'll kill 'em. Right, guys?"

"He can't pitch both games," Biggie said gloomily. "We play them tomorrow and again on Monday."

PAY-OFF PITCH

"Hex will take 'em Monday," Soapy said stoutly. "Wait and see."

The A & M game was as thrilling to the Statesmen as a World Series game is to an avid major-league fan. So on Saturday, when State opened its crucial two-game series against the Aggies with second place in the conference at stake, the stands were packed.

Rockwell started Chip on the mound and Soapy behind the plate, and the game quickly developed into a pitchers' battle. The big Aggies pitcher was fast and good, and Chip had never felt better. The pitching duel continued right on through the top of the ninth, and when the Statesmen came to bat in the last of the ninth, nothing but goose eggs decorated the scoreboard.

Soapy was at bat, Chip was on deck, and Russ Merton was in the hole. Rockwell let the hitting order ride, but he did grab Soapy's arm long enough to tell him to "look 'em over."

To Soapy, that meant only one thing: get on base! The redhead had caught a beautiful game and singled in the sixth for one of State's five hits. Now he crowded the plate, crouched over the strike zone, baited the pitcher for all he was worth, and worked the count to three and two. Then the Aggies hurler delivered a low fastball that came in around Soapy's knees. Soapy started his swing but stopped his bat at the last second, and the umpire called it ball four. So Soapy was on, and Chip was up.

Chip had batted from the lefty's batting box all through the game. Now with Soapy on first base, he decided to bat righty. He knew what the sign would be and was not surprised when Corrigan called for the advance play. Rockwell wanted Soapy on second base.

The A & M infielders were up on the grass and

prepared for the bunt. Chip looked at the first pitch, a fast sizzler that went for a ball. The next pitch was across the letters. Chip laid it down along the third-base path and sprinted for the base. The visitors' hot-corner guardian was right on top of the perfect bunt, but Soapy was nearly to second base. The only play to make was at first. At that, Chip was nipped only on the last stride.

Chip trotted back to the dugout. Now it was up to Merton and Minson. Merton drilled a hard fly ball just to the right of third base. For a second it looked as if the ball was tagged for extra bases, but the brilliant Aggies third baseman speared the speeding ball and chased Soapy back to second with a lightning peg.

Rockwell called time then, left his third-base coaching position, and headed for the dugout. "Schwartz!" he called. "Hit for Minson."

Once again the veteran coach was calling on one of his high school players in a clutch situation. It was the right choice or hunch; Schwartz laid into the very next pitch and lined the ball over second base and out toward right-center field. Soapy was on his way with the hit, and Rockwell waved him home. It was close, but the redhead beat the throw by a yard. Schwartz's clutch hit had won the game for State and placed the Statesmen in a tie with A & M for second place in the conference. The score: State 1, A & M 0.

It was a great victory, and every player on the team felt a tremendous lift. Now everything depended on winning the Monday game. But that night all hopes of a chance for the conference championship went out the window. Southwestern took a doubleheader from Brandon to clinch first place and the title. The two wins brought Southwestern's season record to twenty-one victories and two defeats—with one game left to play against State the following Wednesday.

PAY-OFF PITCH

The game with A & M on Monday was another pitchers' duel. Rickard was on the mound with Engle behind the plate, and the Aggies' number-one hurler was working for A & M.

State finally scored a run in the seventh inning to break the scoreless tie and take a 1-0 lead. In the top of the eighth, with two down, the A & M pitcher drove a low liner right back to the mound. The crack of the bat was echoed by the crack of the ball against Rickard's leg. The ball went flying as Rickard tumbled to the ground, writhing in pain. The hitter advanced to second base before Engle recovered the ball and called time.

Rockwell was out of the dugout almost as soon as Rickard fell to the ground. "Warm up, Chip!" he cried as he ran toward the field. "Fast!"

Chip warmed up in front of the dugout while watching the scene on the mound. He groaned audibly as Rockwell turned and called for a stretcher. "Not again!" he cried. "Not another one!"

But it was. Hector Rickard's ankle was broken.

Chip took his warm-up throws and then faced the Aggies' leadoff hitter, the third baseman. Chip got him on a foul tip, a called strike, and a fastball that blazed past a full swing for the third strike.

State couldn't score in the bottom of the eighth, and when Chip walked out to the mound in the top of the ninth, the Statesmen were still leading 1-0. That lone tally looked big when Chip struck out the number-two hitter and got the number-three batter on a grass cutter from Crowell to Biggie. That left the Statesmen one out away from second place in the conference.

The cleanup hitter stepped into the box, and Chip got ahead of him, one and two. Then Engle called for a sinker. Chip blazed it out and down, and the batter missed the ball by a foot.

But so did Engle!

The ball skipped along the ground to the grandstand, and the runner stopped on first base. It was Engle's error, but the big receiver was furious when he came back to the plate.

"Come on!" he cried, firing the ball back to Chip with all his strength. "Keep 'em up!"

With the count at two and none on the next batter, the runner tried to steal second. Engle had the runner by a mile. But he fired the ball high over Crowell's head. Fireball made the stop behind second, and his throw was dead on a line to the plate. Chip cut off the throw and held the runner at third base.

The next hitter walked slowly up to the plate and dug in. Chip slipped a fastball past him for a strike, wasted a hook to the outside, and dealt a slider that broke a split second too soon. The call was two balls and one strike. Chip's next pitch was tight inside and close to the wrists, and the hitter got a piece of it, sending the ball up in the air right in front of the mound. It was an easy third out, and Chip called, "I've got it! I've got it!"

Biggie sprinted toward the plate and called, "Chip! Chip's ball! Take it, Chip!"

Al Engle snatched off his mask and was running at full speed right up the alley toward the mound. Biggie reached the plate and covered while Russ Merton, coming in from third base to back up the play again, yelled, "Chip! Chip's got it!"

Chip was concentrating on the ball. Just as he lifted his hands to take the ball, Engle plowed into him. The two teammates crashed to the ground. Chip was wholly unprepared. He never knew what hit him until he was flat on his back with Engle sprawled on top of him.

The ball bounded away, and the runner on third dashed in to tie the score, 1-1. The batter had loafed down toward first base, but when he saw the collision, he turned on the speed and pulled into second base just in time to beat Minson's throw to Crowell.

Biggie called time, but the damage was done. When Chip scrambled to his feet, Rockwell had an arm around Engle and was holding him up. Engle held both hands to his jaw, moaning in pain.

Dr. Mike Terring joined them immediately and quickly examined the injured player's jaw. "Looks like a fracture, Rock," he said. "Come on, Engle. I've got to get you to the medical center."

Engle was hurt, but he still managed to shoot a scowl of enmity in Chip's direction. "It was my play, hero," he growled. "I hope you're satisfied now. Your buddy's got home plate to himself."

Soapy replaced Engle, and Chip got the next hitter on three straight strikes. So it was a tie ball game when the Statesmen came in for their licks in the bottom of the ninth. Biggie led off, and the A & M pitcher was careful to keep his pitches low and outside against the big left-handed hitter. But with the count at three and one, Biggie caught a low outside pitch with the meaty part of his bat.

Chip was up and out of the dugout with the smack of the bat. He knew Biggie had tagged that pitch and that it was a solid blow. Biggie pulled it hard for the right-field fence. The ball took off high and lazy and kept right on going—up and out and over the fence for a home run. Biggie had pulled through, and State had defeated A & M 2-1 to clinch the runner-up spot in the conference.

CHAPTER 17

Throw In with the Hero

AL ENGLE was there when the Statesmen dressed for the final game with Southwestern. But he didn't suit up. He wore a brace around his neck that fitted closely around his chin to protect his fractured jaw. Sitting in front of his locker, he gloomily watched his teammates dress for the game. When Chip came in, he walked over to the injured catcher. It was the first time he had seen Engle since the game on Monday. "I'm sorry, Al," he said.

"Beat it!" Engle growled through clenched teeth. "I'll bet you're sorry!"

Doogie Dugan was standing nearby. "Come on, Al," he urged. "Forget it."

"That figures," Engle rasped, speaking with difficulty. "You *would* throw in with the hero."

"That's not right, Al," Dugan said softly. "It wasn't Chip's fault."

"Oh, no?" Engle rasped. "*Everything's* his fault. He chased Wilder out of school and cost us the conference championship. If it wasn't his fault, whose fault was it?"

"Wilder's fault! His own stupid fault," Dugan said shortly, turning back to his locker.

Engle glared uncertainly at Dugan and then stalked out of the room. The little exchange did not go unnoticed. Most of the players had noticed the coolness between Engle and Dugan since Wilder departed, but they had been unaware of Engle's grudge against Chip.

Chip had avoided Engle since the last A & M game, and the surly catcher had not had an opportunity to press his dislike. Now, as Chip dressed, the warmth and friendliness of the other players toward one another contrasted sharply with the coolness between Engle and himself. "It's too bad," he muttered.

The locker room emptied quickly, and Chip put all thoughts of Engle out of his mind. This was a big game, even though it had no bearing on the championship. Competing against the champion is a thrill in any sport, and Chip was as eager as the rest of the team to test his ability against Southwestern. "I hope I get the chance," he whispered to himself.

Soapy was waiting with his big glove in front of the dugout, a wide grin on his face. "We're it, Chipper, baby!" he cried. "C'mon. Loosen up the old flipper."

Up in the stands, Jim and Cindy Collins shared a bag of peanuts and chatted with the fans, who commented on the Statemen's great season and the hard luck that had cost them the championship. "Good thing this is the last game," one fan said. "Rockwell's only got one catcher left."

"How about the pitchers?" another questioned.

"I never saw anything like it. They started off with four catchers and six pitchers, and now there's only one catcher and one pitcher."

"How about that little guy? The junior college pitcher."

"Dugan? He hasn't started a game yet."

"Only pitched about half a dozen relief innings so far."

State ran out on the field just then, and the fans ceased talking and concentrated on the game. Southwestern had a number of all-conference players on its roster, and could they ever hit! Chip had trouble all through the game, although he held them to four hits. And when State came in to bat in the bottom of the ninth, Southwestern led, 3-1.

It was time for the Statesmen's last bats of the season, and the fans were imploring them to get going and win the game.

"It's now or never, guys!"

"Come on, Minson! Start the ball rolling!"

Minson walked, Russ Merton drove a hard grounder between short and third for a clean single, and Fireball struck out. Biggie came up to bat with runners on first and second and one down. Then, with the count at two and one, Biggie stepped into an inside pitch and pulled it high and away over the right-field fence, in almost the identical spot of his four-bagger against A & M.

The fans practically tore down the bleachers when the ball disappeared over the fence. And when Biggie crossed home plate, a horde of joyful fans and teammates met him.

That was it!

State had upset the conference champions, 4-3!

Chip and Soapy met Biggie at the plate but had to fight to get close enough to shake his hand. Biggie was still surrounded when they elbowed through the mob of fans and players and headed for the locker room.

PAY-OFF PITCH

The fans tried to find Chip a little later, but he and Soapy had disappeared. They tried again that night at Grayson's, but Chip kept busy in the stockroom and left it to Soapy and Fireball to take the bows.

Chip was greatly relieved that the season was over, but he also felt a twinge of sadness. Engle's bad luck and bitterness toward him had hurt. Thoughts of Widow Wilder prompted a review of the season. *He could have been the difference,* Chip mused to himself. *Just as Engle said, Wilder could have meant the championship for State baseball, if he had not been a pro.*

Perhaps it was coincidence. When Chip and Soapy got home to Jeff that night, a letter was lying on the desk. Soapy picked it up and examined the envelope curiously.

"It's for you," Soapy said, handing the letter to Chip. "It's postmarked Alaska."

"I don't know anyone there," Chip said as he opened the envelope. There were two scrawled pages. Chip turned the second one over and stared in surprise at the signature. "Widow Wilder!" he said. "That's funny."

"What's funny about hearing from him?" Soapy demanded. "It can't be anything good."

"I guess not," Chip said, sitting down at the desk. While he read the letter, Soapy flipped on the stereo and flopped down on his bed to wait for Chip to finish.

Soapy was right. It wasn't good. Wilder had written a sad, disillusioned letter. Jon Hart had lined up a great team that played every day, sometimes twice a day. But then, one day, Wilder slid into second base and broke his leg. Hart took him to a hospital.

"That wasn't so bad, Chip," Wilder wrote, "but he just dropped me off and left. He didn't leave me any money to pay the hospital bill or even my way home. He said that since I didn't technically work for the fishing company, I wasn't covered by their insurance plan like some of the other players who truly worked for the company were. And since I'd withdrawn from school, I didn't have any medical insurance at all. Chip, he just left me there and wouldn't even return my calls."

"Naturally," Chip murmured.

"Naturally what?" Soapy asked.

"Well," Chip said thoughtfully, "Wilder's had some bad luck."

"How bad?"

"Pretty bad. He broke his leg."

"Playing ball?"

Chip nodded. "That's right. Here, read the letter."

Soapy read the rest of the letter aloud. "'Someday I'll catch up with him, Chip. Anyway, my parents dug up the money and wired it to me. So I'll be out of here in a day or two, and then I'm coming home.

"'You were so right about everything, Chip. You see, way down at the bottom of the contract I signed, there was a clause that said my bonus would be forfeited if I suffered any kind of injury that would prohibit me from playing ball within ten days after sustaining it. I never saw that.

"'So I'm on my way home, out of baseball, out of college, and out of luck. I wish I had listened to you. But it's too late now. I'm going to try to go to another college this fall. I wish it could be State so I could prove to all the guys—and especially you—that I'm not entirely a washout.'"

"Maybe it's not too late," Chip muttered.

"What's not too late?"

"Nothing, Soapy. By the way, I don't think we should tell anyone else about Wilder's bad luck."

Soapy nodded. "You're right, Chip. I don't like him, but I wouldn't want to hurt him while he's down."

"Well," said Chip, "now that we're through with baseball, we can do a little extra studying."

"We're not through yet. We've got to turn in our uniforms tomorrow afternoon."

"That's right! I forgot about the uniforms. Come on, let's call it a day."

Tired as he was, Chip couldn't get Widow Wilder out of his thoughts. Before he went to sleep, he made up his mind to see Dean Murray as soon as possible.

Right after his first class the next morning, Chip walked over to the dean's office. He got an immediate appointment, much to his relief. He had seen Dean Murray several times, but this was the first time he had ever talked to him personally.

Dean Murray looked up from his desk with a smile when Chip entered his office. Then he rose and extended his hand. "Congratulations, Hilton. I saw the game yesterday. You were magnificent. It's too bad we couldn't have gotten off to a better start early in the season. I think we would have ended up on top, ahead of Southwestern. I guess we can credit—or I should say discredit—Mitch Wilder for that."

"That's what I wanted to talk to you about," Chip said nervously. "You see, sir, I wanted to ask you to give him another chance."

"That's impossible, Chip. He was dismissed."

"I know, sir. But from a legal point of view he did nothing wrong; that is, as far as State is concerned. You see, he never competed for State after he signed the contract or after he played professional ball."

"What about last year?"

"He didn't play pro ball before last year, sir."

Dean Murray eyed Chip speculatively and smiled. "You are aware, naturally, that he wouldn't be permitted to play sports here."

THROW IN WITH THE HERO

"Yes, sir. I know that. He's interested only in coming back to school."

The dean nodded. "I see. Well, I guess I'll have to agree with you—legally. Morally, he hasn't a leg to stand on. He lied to everyone, and he jeopardized the players, the team, and the school."

"But he realizes his mistake, sir. If you read this letter, you'll understand."

Dean Murray read the letter and then leaned back in his chair and studied the ceiling. From time to time he glanced out the window and then shifted his eyes back to the ceiling. Chip watched him, half-convinced that the administrator had forgotten his presence.

"All right," Dean Murray said suddenly, dropping forward and placing his arms on the desk. "I'll think it over. It will be against my better judgment, but I can't overlook your interesting discovery, or should I say presentation, of the legal loophole. I wish all our students were as thoughtful and forgiving as yourself.

"You are perhaps unaware," Dean Murray continued slowly, choosing his words carefully, "that I know a great deal about Wilder. For instance, I know that he tried to get you to join him in that summer ball fiasco. That he tried to get you to agree to a summer job on paper when you'd really be getting paid to play ball. And I happen to know that he started a lot of false rumors about you when you turned him down. I'm glad you are big enough to forgive him."

"It didn't amount to anything, sir."

"I think it did. Anyway, suppose you see me tomorrow at three o'clock. I'll have a decision about Wilder by that time."

That afternoon, when Chip arrived at the field house, the players were lined up to turn in their uniforms. Al Engle was also near the end of the line. Doogie Dugan was sitting on a bench nearby and quietly waiting his turn. Chip got his equipment and fell in beside Ted Ryder. Soapy and Biggie and the rest of his friends were farther ahead in the line.

Engle turned stiffly toward Chip. "We'd be on our way to Texas for the national tournament if you hadn't snitched on Wilder," he sniped, his anger overcoming the pain of speaking.

Chip was surprised but ignored the words. Engle was clearly in a rage. "Anyway, Widow had the last laugh," Engle continued, clearing his throat. "He's in Alaska, playing ball, and he's all lined up to play in South America next winter. Then, after that, Hart says he's sure he can get Widow into the players' draft for the major leagues."

The room had quieted, and every player was listening as Engle went on. "You wanted to make sure your redheaded buddy was able to earn his letter, right? So you told a lot of lies about Widow and got him thrown out of school."

"That's not true," Chip said quickly. "I never told lies about Wilder or anyone else. In fact, I never talked about Wilder to anyone. I never even knew for sure that he was in violation of the NCAA rules until I read it in the paper."

"I know better," Engle rasped. "He saw you sneaking out of Rockwell's house almost every night. And how about the letters? The notes? I suppose *you* didn't write them—"

"No, I didn't!"

There was a slight shuffle as Doogie Dugan moved to stand in front of Engle. "I think I can clear up who wrote the letters, Al," he said clearly.

"You? What do you know about them?"

"Everything!" Dugan said shortly. "I wrote them!"

CHAPTER 18

In the Tournament

DOOGIE DUGAN moved away from Engle and faced his teammates, glancing from one to another. The shock of his words held every player in the room speechless, and the sudden stillness was broken only by the shuffling of feet as the baseball players shifted positions to get a better view of Dugan.

"Yes," Dugan continued, "I wrote the notes to the coach and to the newspaper and to the NCAA."

Engle swallowed hard, slowly shook his head, and managed to voice a few words. "But why? What for?"

"Because Widow didn't care whether he got the school in trouble or not. And because he could have ruined the team and the season for a lot of great guys like Chip and Hex and the rest of our teammates."

Dugan took a deep breath and then continued. "You're wrong about Wilder's situation too. I happen to know that he's had a lot of bad luck since leaving school. And another thing! Wilder knows I wrote the notes."

PAY-OFF PITCH

Engle was still bewildered. "How do you know?"

"Simple. I told him. I told him all about it."

Dugan faced all the players as he said, "Maybe it seems underhanded or unethical to you, but I didn't know what else to do. Widow had told me about his deal—you know, not really working but getting paid as if he were. I knew what that meant. And *he* knew it too. He knew he was getting paid for playing ball. And that's pro no matter how you try to fancy it up with language. I was with him when he met Jon Hart. I wouldn't blame you for thinking I'm pretty despicable—"

"No, wait," Bill Bentley interrupted. "You did the right thing, Doogie. How about it, guys?"

There wasn't any question. Dugan's teammates crowded around him, shook his hand, and patted him on the back. Al Engle quietly moved up to the equipment window and turned in his uniform. Then, all alone, he left the room.

After turning in their uniforms, Chip and his friends walked to Grayson's, talking the whole way about the sudden turn of events. As usual, Soapy was the most talkative one in the bunch.

"That took a lot of guts," Soapy commented, nodding his head in admiration. "Standing up there before all the guys and admitting something like that."

"Well, it certainly cleared Chip," Fireball added.

"Nobody thought Chip had anything to do with those notes," said Biggie.

"Engle did, man," Speed corrected.

"Well," Soapy continued, "Dugan's little speech took care of that. Now maybe he'll lay off Chip."

"He never bothered me," Chip said slowly. "I'm just sorry he got off on the wrong track."

"Let's talk about something else," Biggie suggested

as the group swung through Grayson's Main Street doors. "Right now I'm thinking about devouring one of your Soapy Smith Super Specials. Make me something really big and chocolatey and gooey with whipped cream and nuts. Can you do that, Soapy?"

Chip's Friday classes kept him busy until 2:30 in the afternoon. He left his last class and took a walk along the campus lake. When he came to the administrator's office, it was one minute to three o'clock. Dean Murray was waiting for him and motioned to a chair.

"You're right on time, Hilton. Sit down. I think I've got some good news for you. The probation committee has agreed to give Wilder another chance."

"That's great, Dean Murray. I know you won't be disappointed."

Dean Murray smiled. "I hope you're right," he said. "By the way, I sent a special delivery letter to his parents just a few minutes ago."

Chip thanked the dean again and started for the door. But he stopped when the administrator said, "Oh, I forgot. Good luck in the tournament."

Chip stared for a moment. What was the dean thinking about? Chip was sure the dean was mixing him up with someone else. "Yes, sir," he said. "Thank you, sir."

After leaving Dean Murray's office, Chip took his time on the long walk to Grayson's. He was reliving the season in his thoughts, thinking of all the little tragedies that had handicapped the team and kept his teammates from the success they so richly deserved. "Just one player," he murmured. "The one bad apple mom always said could ruin the entire barrel. Anyway, Wilder will have another chance."

Then he got to thinking about Wilder's love for baseball. He figured that maybe the future wouldn't be so dark for the big receiver after all. Widow's experience as a catcher would be a fine recommendation for a high school coaching position. A teacher seldom got rich, but his life was full of meaningful rewards.

Then Chip got to thinking about himself. He wondered what the future held for him. It was tough to look over one's shoulder at the end of a season or a school year. Tough to think of the wonderful days that were gone forever and to realize the mistakes and deeds that could never be changed.

Grayson's was just ahead, and Chip quickened his pace. Now he could concentrate on his job and repay George Grayson for his generosity in adjusting Chip's work hours around practice and the games. "I'm going to turn that stockroom upside down," he told himself. Hurrying forward, he walked through the State Street entrance, eager to get started but completely unprepared for the chaos inside.

Their faces wreathed in smiles, Mitzi Savrill and George Grayson were standing near the cashier's desk, watching a crowd of fans who jammed the store.

Soapy was standing on a chair behind the fountain and making some kind of speech, and Fireball and Whitty were right behind him. The fans were pressed close together to listen, and every time the redhead finished a sentence, they cheered with such force that Chip's ears began to ring.

Chip could see Biggie, Red, Speed, Doogie, and Bill Bentley up in front, forming a ring to hold back the crowd. Every inch of space was taken up by the cheering, boisterous crowd. Chip paused in astonishment. *What's going on?*

Then Soapy saw him. "And now," the redhead shouted, pointing dramatically toward Chip, "I give you the man who made it possible—the hungry hurler who won eleven straight games and put us in the NCAA tournament, Chip Hilton!"

The fans turned and converged on Chip, yelling, "Speech! Speech! Speech!"

Chip fought them off, trying to figure out what Soapy had said about a tournament. *What tournament?*

The happy fans pushed him around behind the fountain until he was standing beside Soapy. Chip grabbed Soapy by the arm. "Hey, Soapy! What's this all about?"

That was the cue for Soapy. He studied Chip for an amazed second and then turned to the crowd and held up his hands for silence. "Hey! Hold it!"

Soapy put his arm around Chip's shoulder and gestured for silence. "Listen! Get this! This will kill you! Chip wants to know what it's all about. He doesn't even know we're in the tournament!"

Everyone in the store tried to tell Chip, and the result was a garbled, wisecracking cacophony of sound. But just enough meaning filtered through from the fans and Soapy's jubilant shouts for him to learn that State had been invited to participate in the NCAA tournament. The team was leaving for Texas Saturday afternoon.

"I don't believe it!" Chip cried out. "Who are you trying to kid?"

"We're not kidding!" Soapy yelled. "We're flying out of here tomorrow afternoon for Austin, Texas. Woo-eee! Where's my cowboy hat?"

Chip was still confused. "No way!" he said, struggling to get away from Soapy's grasping hand. "You're crazy!"

"Here!" someone in the crowd yelled, shoving a copy of the *Herald* up to Chip. "Look at that headline!"

There it was! Right on the first page of the sports section. A banner headline extended clear across the page in big, bold letters:

PAY-OFF PITCH

STATE TO PLAY IN NCAA TOURNAMENT

Chip tried to read more, but it was impossible. Soapy grabbed the paper and sent it sailing over his shoulder. "Now do you believe it?" he yelped. "Hold it, everyone! Hold it! Chip's going to make a speech!"

The crowd quieted, waiting for Chip to begin. He shook his head and glared sideways at Soapy. "I'll get you for this," he said, shaking a fist under the redhead's nose. He turned to face the fans.

"This is all news to me. I still don't know what happened. But if that headline is true, I'm sure happy."

In the thunder of applause that followed, Chip leaped to the floor and picked up the paper. He elbowed his way through the crowd and headed to the stockroom. On the way, he could hear his excited roommate explaining how State had beaten Southwestern. Amused, Chip paused to listen at the stockroom door.

"You see, it was like this," Soapy said expansively. "Here we are in the bottom of the ninth. Chip has pitched a bea-u-tiful game, but we're behind in the score. Biggie is up there at the plate, so I wink at Rockwell, he's the coach, you know.

"And I walk out there and call time, and I beckon to Biggie. And when he gets real close, I whisper real secretive-like in his ear. I whisper, 'Hit the next pitch out over first base, Biggie. They've got only one man playin' in right field!'

"Then I get another inspiration, and I say, 'Look, Biggie, let's not take any chances! Even that one man out there in right field is a threat to our plan.' And Biggie says, 'That's what I was thinking. What will we do?' And I say, 'Hey, I know! Hit it over the fence!'

"And you know what? *He did it!*"

IN THE TOURNAMENT

Soapy's grand finale evoked a thunderous roar of laugher and applause. Chip slipped inside the stockroom and closed the door, spreading the *Herald* on his desk to read the headline again. It was true. There was no doubt about it. There it was in print, the whole story. Now he understood Dean Murray's comment about having good luck in the tournament!

STATE TO PLAY IN NCAA TOURNAMENT
Locals Replace Southwestern;
Southwestern Stars Ruled Ineligible

A statement issued this morning confirmed that State University will compete in the NCAA tournament.

Three of Southwestern's baseball stars were ruled ineligible by the conference eligibility committee because they were in violation of NCAA rules. The three athletes admitted they had been paid to play baseball last summer. Consequently, Southwestern's conference victories were ruled invalid and the team was stripped of its NCAA invitation.

State University was moved up a notch in the final standings and declared the conference and sectional champions.

There was more, but that was enough for Chip. He slouched back in his chair, completely overcome by the near disaster that had escaped State and the unbelievable good fortune that now enveloped his team. It was a dream come true.

CHAPTER 19

Sudden-Death Series

UNIVERSITY AIRPORT was jammed Saturday afternoon. University fans and State's faculty and students carried red-white-and-blue State U. pendants and gave their heroes a great send-off. The crowd was yelling, cheering, and applauding for the coaches, players, trainers, and managers as they walked down the concourse to their gate.

While waiting at the edge of the crowd, Fireball Finley slipped a small diamond ring on Cindy Collins's finger and kissed her.

Speed Morris, who was standing nearby, shook his head in amazement. Sidling up to Biggie, he nodded in the couple's direction and declared, "Only a baseball player on his way to seizing an NCAA title would think an airport was romantic enough for a proposal."

And then all the friends surrounded the couple and offered their best wishes. Chip and Fireball's eyes met and held for a brief moment.

Soapy led the way up the jetway with Chip close behind him. As he stepped into the plane, Soapy elbowed Chip and jerked his head toward the female flight attendant standing near the cockpit. She was a very pretty young woman—not much older than Soapy—but the best was yet to come. Up ahead, standing just inside the coach bulkhead, was the most attractive girl Chip had ever seen.

"Oh, man," Soapy said, gulping. "Do I ever love airplanes!" He turned and beckoned eagerly for Chip to follow.

"Can I help you? What's your seat number, sir?" the flight attendant asked, misreading Soapy's "frozen in the headlights" look.

"It's Soapy Smith," Soapy sputtered quickly. "And this is Chip, Chip Hilton."

She grinned. "Your seat number is Soapy Smith, is it?"

Oblivious, Soapy pointed to the nametag on her uniform. "You must be Candy Sweet," he stuttered, "er, I mean Candy Gray."

"That's right," the attendant said briskly, "I'm Ms. Gray. Now how about you just take your seat, Mr. Soapy Smith, and fasten your seat belt. And no smoking!"

"Smoking!" Soapy repeated indignantly, throwing back his shoulders and sticking out his chest. "Lady, I mean, Ms. Candy, we're not allowed to smoke, and we wouldn't if we could! You see, we're athletes. We're the national baseball champions. I mean, well, we will be this time next Saturday."

"I know," Candy Gray said sweetly, "and you're the star pitcher."

"Oh, no, Ms. Gray. You're wrong. I'm a catcher, and I'm only a sophomore."

"There never was any doubt about that," the flight attendant said laughingly. "Tell me more sometime."

"How about that, Chip?" Soapy said smugly as he settled himself in his seat next to the window. "She practically asked me for a date."

"Oh, sure," Chip agreed. "Maybe we'd better change seats."

"Right! Maybe I can help serve the chow or the coffee or the milk or the tea or the Coke or the pillows or the aspirin or the—"

"OK, but don't bother me," Chip said, fastening his seat belt. "I want to sleep."

"Not me," Soapy said. "I've got a hankering for something. Something sweet. I think maybe it's candy."

"Don't forget Mitzi."

Soapy slumped down in his seat. "Man, Chip, you would say that," he groaned, adjusting his seat belt as he did so. "Now you've spoiled everything. I guess I'll go to sleep too."

It was midnight when the team arrived in Austin, and Rockwell hustled the players right to their hotel. They went to church in the morning, and in the afternoon Rockwell took them for a long walk. When Chip and Soapy got back to the hotel, Soapy bought every newspaper in sight.

Back in their room, the redhead skipped from paper to paper looking for something about State. "Here it is, Chip. The story and the draw sheet. Read it."

Chip read the story while Soapy studied the pairings.

CRIPPLED STATE TO MEET TEXANS
Texans Favored in Tournament Opener

The first game in the National Collegiate Baseball Championship tournament will be played tomorrow afternoon at Austin Field by State University and Texas State. Northwest and Southern have drawn byes.

SUDDEN-DEATH SERIES

On Tuesday, Mill University faces California Tech. The top-bracket winners will meet Northwest Wednesday morning, and the lower-bracket winners will meet Southern in the afternoon. The winners of the semifinal round will meet for the national championship Thursday afternoon.

They exchanged papers when Chip finished the story. Soapy was worried. "Here's the draw sheet, Chip. It's a sudden-death tournament, all right. You lose one and you go home. Period!"

"Then we've got to win."

"Who do you think Rock will pitch tomorrow? You or Dugan?"

"I don't know. It's a tough decision. If we had just one more pitcher—"

"I hope he uses you," said Soapy. "At least we'll have one game in the bag. I wish you could pitch 'em all."

Chip smiled. "I'd like to give it a try. One thing is for sure."

"What?"

"You'll have to catch them all."

Soapy grinned. "That suits me fine. Oh, man, who would have thought a week ago that we'd be playing for the national championship?"

"Not me."

Soapy picked up the draw sheet again. "You know, Chip, Northwest is the tough team. Rock might use Dugan tomorrow and save you for Wednesday. You know why?"

"Nope."

"Well, if Dugan gets into trouble tomorrow, he could use you as a relief pitcher and still start you on Wednesday. Aw, it's too much for me. I'm glad it's Rock's problem."

Chip was studying the pairings. There was a lot of baseball ahead in just five days.

"Well," Soapy demanded when Chip finished, "what do you think?"

"It's a big job for two pitchers and one catcher."

"One pitcher," Soapy corrected. "Dugan's pitched exactly twelve innings in twenty-four games."

"That can't be right—"

"Oh, no? Listen. He started the A & M game, and you had to bail him out with the score tied and the bases loaded. Right?"

"I guess so."

"Then he took your place in the Wilson U. game in the eighth when we had 'em four to nothing. You tell me the other games he played in."

"I guess that's it."

"Sure that's it," Soapy declared. "He's only been in two games."

"He hasn't had much of a chance, Soapy."

"I sure hope he's got more than he's shown. If he hasn't, we're out of luck."

"You know what Rock said this afternoon! Let him do the worrying and win 'em one at a time."

"Right! C'mon, We'll be late for dinner."

Rockwell took the players to a movie after dinner. Then he led them on a long, leisurely walk and sent them to bed.

Monday dawned clear and hot. When the team got to the field that afternoon, it was perfect baseball weather.

Soapy wasn't psychic, but his guess that Rockwell would start Doogie Dugan in the first game was correct. And, as if by remote control, the game went as Soapy had predicted. The State hitters gave the little pitcher a lot of help by scoring five runs on seven hits. But Dugan was in one bad hole after another. Only superb support held the Texans to four runs. In the bottom of the ninth, everything seemed to go wrong.

With the Statesmen leading 5-4, Dugan walked the first batter, putting the tying run on first base. The Texans' second hitter bunted on the first pitch. It was a perfect double-play ball, rolling straight up the alley, but Dugan fumbled the ball and couldn't make the throw. So there were runners on first and second. The Texas State coach played it smart. He called for another bunt, and Dugan fumbled again. That loaded the bases with no one down. Rockwell called time and walked out to the mound.

In the State dugout, Chip, Speed, Schwartz, Durley, and Al Engle were leaning forward, tense with anxiety. Engle had been quiet and subdued on the trip so far. But now he turned to Chip and hissed contemptuously. "Isn't this is a nice spot for you, hero boy. Go on in! Go in and save the game."

Chip ignored the taunt. All he cared about was State's predicament. Rockwell suddenly turned toward the dugout and motioned Chip out to the mound. Chip got his glove and walked slowly toward the diamond, passing Dugan on the way. "Too bad, Doogie," he said as they passed.

"I guess I haven't got it," Dugan murmured.

Chip took his warm-up throws and stepped behind the mound to wait for Soapy's sign. The hitter stepped into the batter's box, and Chip drove a fastball inside, shoulder-high. The batter went for it and popped up over Soapy's head for the first out. The runners were held on base, and that brought up the Texas cleanup hitter.

The mere appearance of the dangerous hitter drew a tremendous cheer from the crowd. Rockwell called time and walked out to the mound once again. "He's had three for four, Chipper, but you've got to pitch to him. Keep 'em low and inside. All right, Chip, you can do it."

Behind him, Chip's teammates were pepping him up. Chip concentrated on following Rockwell's orders. With the count at two and one, the burly hitter went for one of Chip's low curveballs and met the pitch solidly. The ball came back to Chip's glove-hand side so quickly that the eye could not follow its blazing path. Chip had followed through the pitch with his arms dangling and feet spread perfectly. His stab at the ball was instinctive, but it was just right. The ball smacked into his glove, making a perfect echo for the crack of the bat.

The force of the speeding ball sent Chip spinning around in position for a throw to third base. Chip fired the ball toward the bag with all his might, and Minnie Minson moved like a streak of lightning to catch the ball and trap the runner off base by ten feet. The game was over! The score: State 5, Texas 4.

Chip really got a roughing up then. It seemed to him that his teammates had him up on their shoulders before the base umpire had his thumb in the air to signify the third out. They had done it!

Dinner that night could have been a banquet feast or cold stew. It wouldn't have made any difference to the Statesmen. All they could think or talk about was the game and how the victory had put them in the semifinals.

They worked out Tuesday morning, and that afternoon they watched California Tech snow under Mill University, 11-3. And when the Statesmen went to bed that night, they were full of confidence. Chip was slated to pitch against Northwest the following morning, and they were content to follow Rockwell's advice to "leave the worrying to him and win 'em one at a time."

CHAPTER 20

National Championship

STATE UNIVERSITY took the field to start the Wednesday game; an uninformed observer would have thought State was the home team. The Texas fans were now rooting for the Statesmen because they had beaten the locals. When Chip walked out to the mound, he received a tremendous cheer. The fans hadn't forgotten his Monday relief role.

Chip held the Northwest batters to two hits for the first seven innings. Not a runner reached second base. And when the Statesmen got two runs in the bottom of the stretch inning, it looked as if that was all the edge Chip would need.

In the top of the eighth, the first hitter struck out and the second flied out to Fireball. The third batter took a ball and a called strike and then tipped one of Chip's sliders. The ball nipped Soapy's thumb. Chip was halfway to the plate when Soapy grinned and shook it off. "I'm all right, Chipper." He held out his hand to the umpire for another ball. Then he tossed it out to Chip. "It's nothing, Chip. Let's go!"

Chip's next pitch was outside for a ball, making the count two and two. This time Soapy walked two or three strides out in front of the plate and again tossed the ball to Chip. There was a plea for understanding in Soapy's eyes that restrained Chip from saying anything about the thumb.

"He's hurt," Chip whispered to himself. "Bad."

Chip nearly snapped his wrist off on a slider and sighed in relief when the batter missed it for the third strike. Then he hurried along beside Soapy to the dugout. "How is it, Soapy? Let me see."

"No, Chip," Soapy hissed. "Please! Don't let on. It'll be all right. We've only got one more inning." He ducked down into the dugout. Chip let it go.

The Statesmen didn't score in the bottom of the eighth, and when they took the field in the top of the ninth, they still led, 2-0.

While Soapy was putting on his catching gear, Ted "Tubby" Ryder took Chip's warm-up throws. When Soapy was ready, the first Northwest hitter stepped into the batter's box. Soapy didn't let up with the chatter, thumb or no thumb.

Chip got the jump on the batter, and on the zero-and-two pitch drove a fast curve around the hitter's knees. The batter missed the ball, but Soapy couldn't hold the pitch. The ball rolled only a little distance from the plate, and Soapy retrieved it in plenty of time to throw the runner out at first, but he didn't even make the attempt. The crowd rode him hard for that miscue.

The second batter stepped into Chip's first pitch and got hold of it. But the result was a topped ball that stopped dead in front of the plate. Soapy was on it fast enough, and ordinarily he could have cut the second-base runner down easily. He tried it now, but the ball looped up and over Ozzie Crowell's head and on out into center field.

Fireball was caught by surprise and was slow fielding the ball. His hurried throw was wide of the plate, and the runner made it all the way for Northwest's first run of the game. There was no one down, and the tying run was on second base.

Chip held the runner close to second base, but on the first pitch, he broke for third base. The batter missed the outside pitch by a foot, and Soapy should have had the runner by a mile. But he made no attempt to throw the ball. Instead, he handed it to the umpire and called time. Chip rushed up to the plate, and Rockwell ran out to see what was wrong.

Soapy looked down at his thumb and gritted his teeth. "I think it's busted, Coach. I can't throw."

Rockwell escorted Soapy to the dugout and turned him over to the trainer. Then he tried to figure out what to do. Leading 2-1, top of the ninth, no one down, and the tying run on third base. With no catcher left!

Everyone in the park knew about State's run of bad luck; the fans were quietly sympathetic.

"I'll try it, Coach," Ryder offered in hesitation.

Rockwell studied the players on the field. There was no help there. "All right, Ryder. Go ahead."

Chip and Ryder held a short conference about the signs, and Chip threw a couple of pitches to the stubby second baseman. Then the umpire called, "Play ball!" and Chip stepped back off the mound. The batter had walked the first time up, struck out the second time, and fouled out to Biggie the third time.

Chip decided to keep everything low. That was a help to Ryder too. Chip worked the count to two and two and then threw a sinker dead for the center of the plate. Tubby was on his knees when he caught the ball, but he held onto it for the initial out.

The next batter drove a grounder toward second base. Chip was on it like a cat. He fielded it cleanly, faked the throw to Minson, and then threw the runner out at first for the second out. Biggie ran in toward the plate with the ball to hold the runner on third before handing it to Chip. Now the Statesmen were just one out away from the championship game.

When Chip toed the plate to pitch to the next hitter, the runner on third started a dancing act of breaking toward the plate and returning. Chip took his time and concentrated on keeping the ball low. With the count at one and one, the batter cut under one of his fastballs. The foul went spinning high in the air in front of the grandstand.

Chip advanced toward the plate while watching Ryder closely. Tubby was having difficulty getting into position for the catch. He was moving backward, his head pushed far back, as he tried to get under the ball. As the spinning sphere dropped swiftly toward him, Tubby shook his head and blinked his eyes. Then he began to sway, stumbling as he moved to get under the ball.

"He's lost it!" Chip breathed. Acting on impulse, reacting without a second's delay, he sprang forward, pushed Tubby out of the way, and stabbed at the ball.

It was close, but Chip got his glove hand under the ball. He gripped it firmly with both hands. Chip looked at the ball in disbelief for a second. It was the third-out ball, the ball that put State into the championship game. Then he ran toward the dugout.

But he didn't make it. This time it was the fans who rushed Chip. And he didn't get away. It was the second

NATIONAL CHAMPIONSHIP

time the Texans had seen this tall, slender pitching phe-
nomenon make a winning clutch play, and they wanted
to get close to him, to see what he looked like, and to find
out just what kind of a young man he was.

That afternoon, after a quick lunch, Rockwell and
the Statesmen sat in the stands and watched California
Tech beat Southern, 7-3. Now they knew which team
they had to beat. They knew, too, that they were up
against a championship ball club. Tech could hit and field
and had a fine pitching staff.

Rockwell had told them to relax and let him do the
worrying, but now, with the championship in sight, Chip
was tense and fidgety. His thoughts kept jumping ahead
to the following afternoon. The pitching responsibility
rested squarely on the slender shoulders of Doogie
Dugan. Chip would have jumped at the chance to pitch,
but he knew Rock wouldn't consider it. Coach Rockwell
wouldn't let one of his pitchers work without three days'
rest if winning the world championship depended upon
it. It was up to Dugan.

"That's only half of it," Chip murmured. "What are
we going to do for a catcher?"

Soapy's thumb was fractured; he couldn't possibly
play. Engle had suited up for both games, but beyond
that he had played the part of a lone wolf, nursing his
jaw and avoiding everyone, Dugan included.

That night Coach Rockwell sent the team to an early
movie with orders to be in bed by ten o'clock. Chip and
Soapy, too tight to enjoy the film, left before the end of
the movie and slowly walked back to the hotel. Both were
tense and worried. Chip knew Rockwell and his moods.
And he knew that Rock was worried. Soapy knew it too.

"Dugan can't do it, Chip. Rock knows it, and he's all upset. Doogie won't last three innings."

"He's got to last."

"What about Ryder?"

"I don't know, Soapy. He's pretty small, and he hasn't got a very strong arm."

"Chip, we might as well face it. They'll run wild on the bases. And with Dugan pitching," Soapy uncharacteristically spread his hands in resignation, "they'll be running over one another's heels."

"Cut it out, Soapy."

"You know it as well as I do. And so does everyone else. The whole team is upset. We're beat before we start."

"You know the old saying: The game isn't—"

"I know, the game's not over until the last out. We'll be lucky to get 'em out in the first inning."

"We'll see. Let's get some sleep."

The next afternoon, Rockwell waited until the players were all dressed and then got their attention. "This is it, men. It's a tough spot, but we've got to face it. We're playing for the national championship with one pitcher and no catchers. Dugan is set to go, but Tubby doesn't think he can handle the catching."

No one moved in the interim that followed Rockwell's statement. Chip broke the silence. "I'll try it, Coach."

Rockwell thought about it a moment and then shook his head. "No, Chip, I don't like it. You relieved in the Monday game and went all the way on Wednesday. That's enough. No, we'll start with Ryder."

There was a big crowd in attendance for the game. Tech had a senior team and had won the Pacific Coast championship without a single defeat. Los Angeles baseball fans knew that major-league scouts were camped out on the Tech campus and just waiting for the final game so they could approach several of the team's stars about the upcoming draft.

Tubby handled the catching chores during the infield practice, and Chip warmed up Dugan. The little pitcher's chief strengths were his good control and a tricky curve. But it took only a few throws for Chip to realize that Dugan had lost his confidence. He would need a lot of help behind the plate. He glanced out at the infield just as Tubby pegged a ball down to second base. It was a bad throw, flying into the dirt twenty feet in front of the bag, through Crowell's glove, and on out to center field.

Chip shifted his glance to the Tech side of the field. The California coach was out in front of the dugout, his keen eyes taking in every move Tubby made. "He'll run on everything," Chip muttered. "This is bad."

Bad it was! Tech took the field and retired State's Merton, Minson, and Bentley—one-two-three. Then the Statesmen took the field, and the debacle began. Dugan walked the first hitter and hit the second.

On the next pitch, both runners took off on a double steal. It was an outside pitch from Dugan, and Tubby had plenty of time. Too much! He took aim and fired the ball over Minson's head and on out into left field. The first runner scored, and the second was held to third only by Bentley's peg to the plate.

Rockwell ran out of the dugout and onto the field. "Time!" he cried. "Hold everything."

Chip, Soapy, Speed, Red, and Al Engle had followed Rockwell and were standing in front of the dugout. Right then they got a surprise that almost shocked them out of their concern about Dugan and Ryder.

Widow Wilder hobbled down out of the grandstand, escorted by two ushers, and headed straight for Chip.

Engle grabbed at his old friend, but Wilder pushed past him and pounced on Chip.

"Chip!" the big player cried out. "How are you?" He gripped Chip in a bear hug and lifted him up in the air. Then he set him down and greeted the others. "Hi ya, Smith. Hey, Schwartz. Hi, Al—" He stared at the bandage around Engle's neck. "What's wrong with you?"

"Me?" Engle said, "I . . ." He looked from Wilder to Chip and back to Wilder again. "Nothing! What's wrong with *you?* What's with you and Hilton? I thought he was poison to you."

"That's what I thought too," Wilder said. "I was an idiot! You were too. This is the greatest guy I ever met." He draped his arm around Chip's shoulders. "The greatest!"

"You're crazy!" Engle said incredulously.

"Not anymore," Wilder said grimly.

He pulled Chip over in front of Engle. "You know what this guy did?" he said, tapping Engle in the chest. "He got me back in school. I'm coming back to State. In August! And Chip did it. My parents told me all about it. He got Dean Murray to give me another chance."

"You mean you and Hilton are friends?"

"More than that! He's the best friend I ever had."

"What about Dugan and the notes?"

Wilder grinned. "Doogie wrote me all about that. He did the right thing. All the way."

"How about that!" Engle said weakly. "How about that!"

Rockwell was back, followed by Ryder. The worried coach was so engrossed in his problem that he didn't see Wilder. Nodding at Tubby, Coach took the catcher's glove away from Ryder and handed it to Chip. "Here, Chip. You'll have to do it. There's no other way."

NATIONAL CHAMPIONSHIP

Then everyone got a shock. Al Engle pushed between Rockwell and Chip. "Yes, there is, Coach!" he said, turning to Chip. "Give me that glove, Hilton! You're no catcher."

Rockwell turned in startled surprise. "But your jaw—"

"Best thing that ever happened to me," Engle said grimly. "It taught me to keep my mouth shut and do a little thinking."

"But I can't let you."

"You can!" Engle interrupted. "I'm all right."

He put on the chest protector and knelt down to put on the shin guards. "We'll get 'em for you, Coach. You'll see!"

Engle got to his feet and reported. Then he talked briefly to Dugan in front of the plate. Chip and Soapy and a few others saw Al and Doogie grip hands as they stood there earnestly talking. Dugan turned and walked back to the mound and waited for Engle's sign.

Engle squatted behind the plate and gave the sign. "Come on, Doogie, old bud!" he yelled. "You can do it!"

Dugan grinned happily and shook his fist in the air. "*We* can do it!" he yelped.

One of the local stations covering the national championship had planned to interview the victorious players from the field. The crew had set up its gear near home plate. But the dramatic finale of the game brought the fans down from the stands, and they swarmed around the players, making it impossible for the planned interview. The enthusiastic crowd followed the baseball heroes to the dugout. The harried local interviewer with the portable mike tried to push his way through, but he again found himself hopelessly walled off from the champions. Up above the field, the penetrating eyes of the national networks and ESPN cameras captured the scene.

Seconds later, the determined local TV sportscaster found a solution to his problem. With his assistant guarding the long cord, he circled the huge crowd and gained a position on top of the dugout. Fortunately, when the fans below him realized they were on camera, they gave him their full cooperation. As he provided a dramatic summary of the thrilling climax of the game, the fans hoisted the heroes up beside him on top of the dugout. Chip and Soapy were standing right below the announcer and drinking in every word.

"Let me tell you, most of the suspense of this action-packed game was concentrated in the final inning. And now, here's a real ballplayer. As I told you, State came into this final game without a catcher. Coach Henry Rockwell tried to use one of his infielders as a catcher, but it was too much to ask, too much to expect in a championship game. Then, when it looked as if the game would be lost behind the plate, this wonderful player standing here beside me, fractured jaw and all, went into the game and caught every inning."

The crowd's cheer almost drowned out the announcer's words, but he kept right on talking to his viewers.

"That's not all! In the top of the ninth, with two men on base and two down and with California leading 3-2, this great competitor knocked in the tying and winning runs! Now, Al Engle," the reporter continued, "it must have been extremely painful to catch a nine-inning game with a fractured jaw. Why did you do it?"

Engle wasn't in any condition to do much talking, but he gave it a try. "I did it for a great coach and a great team. It was about time I did something. I spent most of the season griping."

The fans didn't know what this was all about, but once again their cheers drowned out the announcer's words. When they quieted down, he continued. "Folks, I guess you know that California Tech was at bat in the last of the ninth, with State leading 4-3 and with two down and the bases loaded.

"And this little guy—I don't think he weighs more than a dozen baseballs—was standing out there facing California Tech's cleanup hitter. Now get this! Get the picture. The count was three and two, and the national championship was at stake. Everything—but everything—depended on one little throw of sixty feet.

"Here he is, fans. Now, Mr. Champion, Mr. Doogie Dugan, what were you thinking about? Tell the fans how you felt out there on the mound in that last big inning. In that last big second! In that crucial moment just before the payoff pitch!"

Dugan looked down at Chip and grinned. "Well, sir," he said, "I was scared to death. Then I heard Chip yelling, and I got to thinking about something he had said."

The announcer stared at Dugan incredulously. "You weren't thinking about the three men on base and the cleanup hitter?"

"No, sir. I was thinking how lucky I was to be on this team, even if I was in a tight spot. And then I remembered what Chip had said. Something I'll never forget. He said that a guy plays baseball because he wants to be a member of a team; he wants to prove he can accept responsibility and that he's man enough to keep trying, even when it looks as if he hasn't got a chance."

"What did he mean by that?"

"Well, I think he meant that a fellow has to work hard, no matter how tough the going is, so that he'll be ready when his big chance comes. This was my big chance to prove I was man enough to face up to a tough spot. And as Chip said, it was sort of a personal challenge. Anyway, I wasn't scared anymore."

"This fellow Chip must mean a lot to you. There must be something personal behind all this."

"There sure is! I wouldn't be standing up here right now if it hadn't been for Chip. I was ready to quit a lot of times during the season, but after I got to know him and what sportsmanship and team play are all about, I learned how to face up to the bad breaks. I just worked as hard as I could and hoped for my big chance. And was it big! I still feel as if it's all a dream."

"It's no dream, Dugan. Now this player—your friend Chip—just who is he?"

"Well, sir, he's the pitcher who won eleven in a row during the season and two of the tournament games. And you saw him cross the plate with the winning run a few minutes ago when Al Engle clouted the ball."

"You mean William Hilton?"

"That's right, except we call him Chip. He's standing right down there. He's the one who really ought to be up here."

"I'll take care of him just as soon as I finish talking with you. Now one more thing, Dugan. There are a lot of young athletes watching and listening to this program. And most of them are about twice your size. What have you got to say to them?"

"The same thing Chip Hilton said, sir: When a player goes out for a team, he should give it all he's got. And whether he makes it or not, he's important and someone pretty special. He's making a big contribution to the team whether he's the bat boy, the manager, or a sub."

The crowd broke again into a deafening cheer, and Chip Hilton was hoisted to the top of the dugout. Flashing Chip a wide smile, Doogie Dugan raised two fingers of his right hand in a V for victory salute as he and Al Engle stepped aside to make room for their teammate and new friend.

Afterword

BEFORE REPLAY AND VCRS, before cable and endless highlight shows, before the almost absurd over-saturation and hype that has distorted the meaning and reduced the magic of sports, it was, in large part, about imagination. The games were on the radio. The images were not imposed and thrust upon you. They came to you more gently, less directly—much of it shaped in the mind's eye, or in a kid's dreams.

As a boy in the '50s and early '60s, I read several of the Chip Hilton stories. What I remember most is how each of them drew me in—the characters, the stories, the anticipation of the climactic game. I always read the last few pages as slowly as possible, reluctant to leave the world I'd so eagerly entered—a world that was simultaneously exciting and reassuring.

Not long ago, a friend mentioned that he had received a few of the reissued Chip Hilton stories as a Christmas gift. He said he'd read them faithfully as a kid. Now, I'd known this guy a long time, but we were just stumbling across this bit of shared history. It had been thirty years since either of us had last opened *Hoop Crazy, Fourth Down Showdown, Strike Three!,* or *A Pass and a Prayer.* Yet, alternately we tossed out the names of the still-familiar characters: Soapy Smith . . . Speed Morris . . . Biggie Cohen . . . Nick Trullo . . . Coach Rockwell.

Clair Bee's stories had obviously left an indelible impression, but just as obviously they came from a very different time and an entirely different set of assumptions about sports and values. We wondered if this stuff would play today, other than as nostalgia for a couple of middle-aged guys like us. So, I put that question to an admittedly unscientific test.

My thirteen-year-old son is an avid sports fan, with an appreciation for history that is uncommon among his peers. Still, he's on the Internet each day. He plays video baseball and football games so high tech they make my boyhood Strat-O-Matic seem like a relic of the dark ages. Could he lose himself in one of these stories, care about it as I once did? I gave him a copy of *Strike Three!*, explaining that I had read it when I was about his age. I told him to read as much or as little of it as his interest warranted.

A day later, he was five chapters in and rattling off the particulars of the plot. Even those references and situations he found dated were amusing to him in a good-natured way. In short, he loved it, and on his own said he would like to read some of the other Hilton books.

Well, how about that? As I said, not a comprehensive survey, but still a pleasant surprise.

AFTERWORD

Maybe someday, he'll be able to make the same statement I'll conclude with: I never met Clair Bee, but I certainly met and felt I knew the people he created, and I still recall the places and events his stories took me to.

BOB COSTAS
NBC Sports

Your Score Card

I have   I expect
read: to read:

_____   _____   1. *Touchdown Pass:* The first story in the series, introduces readers to William "Chip" Hilton and all his friends at Valley Falls High during an exciting football season.

_____   _____   2. *Championship Ball:* With a broken ankle and an unquenchable spirit, Chip wins the state basketball championship and an even greater victory over himself.

_____   _____   3. *Strike Three!* In the hour of his team's greatest need, Chip Hilton takes to the mound and puts the Big Reds in line for all-state honors.

_____   _____   4. *Clutch Hitter!* Chip's summer job at Mansfield Steel Company gives him a chance to play baseball on the famous Steelers team where he uses his head as well as his war club.

YOUR SCORE CARD

I have   I expect
read: to read:

YOUR SCORE CARD

I have   I expect
read: to read:

_____ _____   11. *Fence Busters:* Can the famous freshman baseball team live up to the sports-
writer's nickname, or will it fold? Will big
egos and an injury to Chip Hilton divide the
team? Can a beanball straighten out an
errant player?

_____ _____   12. *Ten Seconds to Play!* When Chip
Hilton accepts a job as a counselor at Camp
All-America, the last thing he expects to run
into is a football problem. The appearance of
a junior receiver at State University causes
Coach Curly Ralston a surprise football
problem too.

_____ _____   13. *Fourth Down Showdown:* Should Chip
Hilton and his fellow sophomore stars be
suspended from the State University football team? Is there a good reason for their
violation? Learn how Chip comes to better
understand the value of friendship.

_____ _____   14. *Tournament Crisis:* Chip Hilton and
Jimmy Chung wage a fierce contest for a
starting assignment on State University's
varsity basketball team. Then adversity
strikes, forcing Jimmy to leave State. Can
Chip use his knowledge of Chinese culture
and filial piety to help the Chung family,
Jimmy, and the team?

YOUR SCORE CARD

I have   I expect
read: to read:

_____   _____   15. **Hardcourt Upset:** Mystery and hot basketball action team up to make *Hardcourt
Upset* a must-read! Can Chip help solve the
rash of convenience store burglaries that
threatens the reputation of one of the Hilton
A. C.? Play along with Chip and his teammates as they demonstrate valor on and off
the court and help their Tech rivals earn an
NCAA bid.

_____   _____   16. **Pay-off Pitch:** Can Chip Hilton and his
sophomore friends, now on the varsity base-
ball team, duplicate their success from the previous year as State's great freshman team
known as the "Fence Busters"? When cliques
endanger the team's success, rumors surface
about a player violating NCAA rules—could it
be Chip Hilton? How will Coach Rockwell get
to the bottom of this crisis? *Pay-off Pitch*
becomes a heroic story of baseball and courage
that Chip Hilton fans will long remember.

About the Author

CLAIR BEE, who coached football, baseball, and basketball at the collegiate level, is considered one of the greatest basketball coaches of all time—both collegiate and professional. His winning percentage, 82.6, ranks first overall among any major college coaches, past or present. His name lives on forever in numerous halls of fame. The Coach Clair Bee and Chip Hilton awards are presented annually at the Basketball Hall of Fame honoring NCAA Division I college coaches and players for their commitment to education, personal character, and service to others on and off the court. Bee is the author of the twenty-three-volume, best-selling Chip Hilton sports series, which has influenced many sports and literary notables, including best-selling author John Grisham.

more great releases from the

Chip Hilton Sports Series

by Coach Clair Bee

The sports-loving boy, born out of the imagination of Clair Bee, is back! Clair Bee first began writing the Chip Hilton series in 1948. During the next twenty years, over two million copies of the series were sold. Written in the tradition of the *Hardy Boys* mysteries, each book in this 23-volume series is a positive-themed tale of human relationships, good sportsmanship, and positive influences—things especially crucial to young boys in the '90s. Through these larger-than-life fictional characters, countless young people have been exposed to stories that helped shape their lives.

WELCOME BACK, CHIP HILTON!

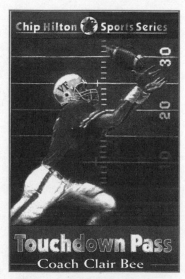

Vol. 1 - Touchdown Pass
0-8054-1686-2

available at fine bookstores everywhere